Rash

Charles Romalotti

Layman Books

Austin   Los Angeles   Glasgow   Auckland   Tokyo

RASH - LAYMAN BOOKS
ISBN: 0-9679235-1-4

Edited by Mark Fagan, Melinda Barsales, and Daniel Smith
Cover art by Daniel Smith
Cover layout design by Dylan Muir, Jaime Hammond, and Daniel Smith
Drawing of Romalotti by Dylan Muir

Available direct-mail from Layman Books for $8

Layman Books
P. O. Box 4702
Austin, TX 78765-4702
www.flash.net/~layman
layman@flash.net

Writing began January 1998, completed October 2000

Release date, June 1, 2001

Printed in the United States by:
Morris Publishing
3212 East Highway 30
Kearney, NE 68847
1-800-650-7888

Thanks goes to the following people for their generous support and critical eye: Yancy Westgate, Ginger Stringer, Josh Muir, Becky Ozuna, Shannan Vaughn, Connie Westgate, Roberta Smith, Lynne York, Gerry and Sarah Kramer, Jesse Casas, Molly Lambert, Heather and Lance Lambert, Tamara Goheen, Sean Davis, Miriam Thompson, Stacy Hoobler, Clarence Smith, Mary Westgate, and Adam Kahan.

for Ginger

SATURDAY, NOVEMBER 7, 1998

Austin, Texas
5:47pm

"Spare some change?" the pavement growled.

Doctor Ronald W. Schtepp stared forward, intent on avoiding eye contact with the rugged youths sprawled along the sidewalk of the Drag. Their dirty bodies were intertwined in a mess of human limbs, enveloped in a deplorably wretched stench. He reached inside the pocket of his polyester pants and jiggled some change, advancing down the stained and broken sidewalk without forfeiting a penny. He enjoyed tormenting them—the ones known locally as the Dragworms. It sickened him how they preyed upon the compassion of liberals and naïve college students. He was safe from their arsenal on both counts.

The cool wind whipped his thinning brown hair into a frazzled mess. His rotund fingers yanked it haggardly in place over his shiny bald crown as he rolled down the sidewalk. His brown vinyl jacket with the tanned elbow patches blended perfectly with the desolate street so aptly named. The cracked pavement was damp from an inconsistent drizzle that made the entire cityscape reek of decay and filth. The murky gray clouds seemed to threaten another chilling shower. He hoped to be inside his cozy Tarrytown home by then.

Strolling past the Church of Scientology, he entered the Bagel Shop on the corner of 22nd Street. Inside, it was warm and empty, as expected. He stepped to the steel counter, catching the eye of the tall man standing rigidly behind it. Their eyes met, and Ronald felt that strange feeling in his chest again. It made him smile, somewhat giddy like a giggly schoolgirl. He liked the feeling.

"Frank," he announced politely to the otherwise silent bakery. His strained voice was prominently male, as though he were advertising after-shave lotion. "What's cookin'?"

Frank Smith raised his eyes and smiled, giving an ambiguous nod. "How are you, Ronald?"

"Not too bad," he decided quickly as he placed his hands passively on the counter's cold metal surface. He gave a proud smile that revealed a row of crooked, yellow teeth. "It's a fine day, though a busy one. It's all about to get much easier, I'm pleased to say. My work with the university is nearing completion."

"The skin stuff?"

2

Ronald smiled with a cocked brow that was as thick as steel wool. "My colleague and I are going to be rich, Frank. This is going to be big—you'll never have to scratch yourself ever again, Frank."

"I kind of enjoy scratching myself..." Frank dropped two pumpernickel bagels in a brown paper bag and lowered it into Ronald's limp, lazy hands. "I'm happy to hear things are moving along finally...I remember how frustrated you were recently. Where did you get the breakthrough, or are you not at liberty to say?"

"No details," Ronald insisted with strict confidence as he placed a dollar and some change on the hard metal counter. "I can tell you that the elusive chemical properties were extracted from known herbal cures." His smile intensified as he paused to reveal the clenching detail that apparently kept him up at night. "The product will be derived from a completely organic origin."

Frank smiled as if he found the subject very riveting. He didn't at all, though. He stood silently, waiting for Ronald to either continue or leave.

Instead, Ronald slouched at the counter obsequiously. "Now, weren't you away recently, Frank?" He stared into Frank's eyes, finding his firm glare to be quite striking. He liked looking into his eyes. In fact, he liked it more than the bagels.

"Had to return to Kansas. Funeral last week."

"Oh...sorry to hear that." His facial expression fell sullen and ill, as if he felt great remorse. He didn't at all, though. "It does happen to the best of us, I'm afraid. Never know when our number is up."

Frank nodded slowly, deliberately withholding any sign of emotion. "Never know."

"Well," Ronald said as he tightly gripped the bag of bagels, "I suppose I should be on my way now. Maybe sometime we could make it out to one of those Ice Bats hockey games...it's a new season, you know."

Frank smiled politely.

"Well...we'll talk about it sometime," Ronald suggested as he removed his wiry glasses to wipe the surface clean. "I wouldn't be against paying."

"I'm kind of busy," Frank began, "with this place."

Ronald nodded, feeling a bit uncomfortable with his forwardness—then he looked into those eyes and knew exactly why he asked. In fact, he knew why he would someday ask again. "Have a good evening, Frank." He stumbled out the side door and down 22nd Street, feeling the cold breeze lapping against his pale, circular face as he staggered humbly to his car.

Pulling up to his quaint little home in Tarrytown, his attention was devoured by a black 1956 Plymouth Fury convertible sitting in front of the house. He paused momentarily, wondering whose it was and how long its presence would be allowed to desecrate his beautifully manicured lawn. He stepped down onto the wet street, locking the doors of his pearly white BMW before waddling proudly up the driveway. He immediately stopped when he discovered a blade of grass resting on the clean cement. He reached down and picked it up, placing it in his coat pocket until he could dispose of it properly.

As he fumbled for his keys, he rummaged through the day's mail. Several bills, and no new copy of *Sports Illustrated.* He loved that magazine, though he never read or understood a word of it. The pictures, he felt, were art. The sweat, the struggle, the passion, the muscles of men colliding... He suddenly felt something rubbing firmly and affectionately against his leg. When he looked down, his eyes met those of his housemate, Adonis. His cat.

"Adonis," he said as he reached down to caress his head. "How did you get out?"

No answer.

He slipped the key inside the lock, twisting it with a limp wrist and no resistance. To his dismay, it wasn't locked. As he pushed the door open, he stood cautiously immobile. No intruders to be seen, only the cold emptiness. The place was just as he left it, spotless and clean. Authentic posters of Broadway musicals were housed in steel frames, secured to the chalky white walls. The thick brown carpet still bore the tracks of the sweeper from earlier in the morning. The artificial scent of lemon was strong, and the atmosphere was painfully cold.

"Silly me," he said to Adonis as he stumbled inside. "Seems I failed to lock the door. I would've forgotten my head if it wasn't attached...are you a hungry kitty?" He pushed through the swivel doors of his bedroom where the walls were painted ice-blue and the bedspread was an appropriate match with patterns of icebergs and penguins. The swivel doors squeaked annoyingly behind him as they closed once again. He removed his coat and placed it amongst his small collection of drab business attire and pastel lingerie. He could smell the fragrance of Shalimar in the frigid air. The scent of Lucinda. The thought of her brought a warm smile.

Adonis meandered between his feet, rubbing passionately, begging for attention.

As he stepped away from the closet, he noticed that a message was flashing on his answering machine, opposite his Queen-sized bed. A picture of his ex-wife towered over the machine. He refused to remove the photograph, if for any other reason than her dress in the picture matched perfectly the pattern on the quilted nightstand.

He pushed through the squeaky swivel doors and lumbered to the kitchen. A strange feeling of discomfort infected his environment, though he spoke what came to mind: "Hungry kitty." As Adonis fed from the tin can that rested in the palm of his hand, he felt a crisply cold draft creep up his spine. He turned quickly, to nothing. Yet, a draft had penetrated somehow, as if a window were open, and that uneasy feeling of being watched... "ESPN tonight, Adonis. Boxing..."

He lowered the tin can to the icy cold counter and crept back to the bedroom. The doors squeaked mercilessly as he passed through them. Someday, he resolved, he would hire some young man with impressive tools to fix that obnoxious squeak. The thought of it brought a mischievous smile. He lowered himself to the bed, avoiding looking at the picture of his ex-wife as he pressed the play button on his answering machine. The caller ID showed it to be his business colleague, Vaughn Richter. He figured as much. No one else calls him.

"Ronald, I need you!" Richter's voice exclaimed desperately, breaking the silence of the cold room. "I need to speak with you—now. Please call me immediately. She's dead. Purty's dead. I've killed her... I don't know what to do..."

His voice faded quickly to silence, leaving a stale chill in the air. Suddenly, like nails on a chalkboard, the sound of the squeaky door sent a tremor of fear through his hefty frame. As he turned, his eyes widened with horror.

"Purty?" he declared fearfully. "Is that...you?" He could barely recognize her to be human. Her rotting skin seemed to drip from her emaciated body. It appeared that she had been skinned, nothing more than a bloodied carcass with the flesh still dangling from slick muscle.

"I want the antidote," she growled. Her bottom lip hung freely as though it was partially severed, making her speech relatively indistinguishable. "Cure me."

"I don't know what you're talking about."

"You don't know?" she hissed.

"No," he replied with a trembling, terrified quaver. "I don't know."

The crackling thunder of gunfire ripped through the room as the bullet penetrated his head, splattering his brains against the wall behind him, splitting his head like cracked watermelon.

This was how Ronald W. Schtepp died.

Sunday, August 16, 1998

Tucson, Arizona
4:03pm

Dirty fingers quickly sifted through the stacks of vinyl records, ignoring any release not of an independent origin. The electronic rhythms of early Industrial music pulsated throughout the Toxic Ranch record store as Jobie Wallace stood alone, immersing himself in a subterranean world of seven-inch singles. His poorly managed long fingernails retained a layer of grime over chipped black nail polish.

He inhaled deeply, absorbing the musty scents of his surroundings. This store was as much his home as anywhere else, though he had never set foot in Tucson until earlier that day. It was the contents of the store rather than its locale, containing the music and literature of the anarchist philosophy that pushed the blood through his young, thin body. He held firm the staunchly liberal beliefs of bands like Naked Aggression and Capitalist Casualties. He considered himself a political advocate, an anarchist with a mission. The only shirt he owned, the one on his back—a sleeveless Crass T-shirt, once black, though now it had a brownish tint from months of filth, displayed proudly his political colors. A large tear zigzagged across his back, sewn haphazardly together with dental floss. The slogan *Fight War, Not Wars* stretched across the back of his shirt, a sort of rally cry to all those who stood behind him. The rest of his outfit was the last of his clothing as well. A plaid flannel kilt draped over his bony legs. It was an image inspired partly by heritage and partly by influence of a punk rock band known as the Real McKenzies. His toes peeked through an ancient pair of combat boots that were wrapped with duct tape to keep his soles intact. He showered infrequently, if ever. He felt people kept their distance based on his ragged appearance. He was mistaken.

The expression on his face was rigid and speculative, by choice. It was part of the uncivil, streetwise image he wished to portray for himself. His bony face was splotchy with acne and razor stubble. Jailhouse-style tattoos of cobwebs spanned from the peak of his nose down across his narrow, pasty cheeks. His hair was short and disorderly, with the left portion dyed black while the right was bleached a stunning white. Despite his adverse sense of style, and to his dismay, his most striking features were those given at birth—piercing icy-blue eyes that could penetrate the coldest of hearts. His smile was very

7

enticing as well, though he chose to restrict such expressions as often as possible. As he saw it, there was no place for smiles in a world so malicious and destructive. Such an expression would be turning a blind eye on the hard truth. Jobie considered smiles the badges of weak and trusting servants of a corrupt and barbaric fascist order. He was proud of the fact that he lived outside the system. He held no job and paid no taxes. He depended on nothing and no one—except those who mercifully supplied their pocket change daily for much needed meals.

The nation's highways were his home, resting nightly on the soil he spurned so adamantly. On his eighteenth birthday, just four months earlier, he and his younger brother Rik left their abusive home life in Tacoma, Washington in favor of freedom and adventure. Jobie's pockets contained a collection of four rocks—one from each state they had traveled to the present. Forty-six remained uncollected.

His other two possessions remained closely at his side—a collection of Noam Chomsky's writings and his own work in progress, *The Apolitical Manifesto*, which was more or less a glorified journal of rhetorical ranting. It was filled with second-hand perspectives on blind consumerism and the corporate censorship of mass media.

His eyes widened and his fingers ceased as he gazed happily at an orange and yellow record. It was a curious sight, the type for which he lived. It was an unknown record from an obscure punk band featured recently in the *Lost Legends* section of *Maximum RockNRoll*. They were called the Jerk Offs—a band that had stumbled briefly onto fleeting notoriety after their vocalist, Norman Malley died tragically over ten years ago. Strangely, this particular seven-inch had a different singer, which wasn't mentioned in the article. He wondered what circumstances buried this portion of the band's history. He often contemplated the fates of these people, the ones who pioneered the vision to which he so passionately subscribed. How did they learn to survive in a world that so radically contradicted the movement's philosophies?

He walked the record to the counter, examining its simple cover art. "I want to listen to this record."

The clerk grudgingly gestured to a stereo with a set of headphones.

"Why does this store carry corporate merchandise?" Jobie asked. "I mean, you have a section for the Media Whores—total sell-outs. Isn't this an independent record store?"

The clerk stared without reply. He had grown tired of responding to Jobie's menial questions and accusations. It was almost as if Jobie sensed a conspiracy, as if there were any other reason to stock a product beyond the general principle of supply and demand. After hours of interrogation, the silent approach seemed to be the best response.

Jobie sneered at him with slit eyes, clearly marking his disapproval. He'd break something before he left.

He carefully placed the record on the player and fastened the headphones over his large ears. The gnawing background noise dissipated behind the crackling pops of the record. He watched the clerk staring at him with contemptuous eyes. Without warning, all his thoughts were devoured by a thick wall of passionate anxiety surging through the headphones. Goosebumps covered his arms as a smile formed across his face, though it was quickly extinguished by his own sense of reason. This was it. That new high, delivered by a recording over a decade old. He lived for such a rush, and hardcore was his drug of choice. Such a pure high, yet only as good as the unfamiliarity of the music. Comprehension brings immunity, carrying with it the craving of a newer, faster, stronger, and harder high. If he could only find a way to steal this record...

A stiff finger tapped him aggressively on the back. He didn't even flinch—he knew it was his brother.

"What?" he asked.

A more aggressive tapping came as a response.

"What?!" He removed the headphones, glancing over his shoulder at a pair of fiery red eyes. Not bloodshot, but candy-apple red—from a pair of artificially colored contact lenses. Red and green eye make-up seemed to explode across his face in a nuclear sunburst. The result was something close to a demon from a B-movie sci-fi flick. His hair was shaved over his ears with the rest extending toward the lighting fixtures in a ratted mess of burnt orange and black. From the neck up, he looked completely and convincingly alien. A skin-tight black mesh shirt hugged his pale and thin body. A black cheerleader skirt fanned out at his hips. Blood red cotton leggings seemed to drip inside patent leather neon-green boots with three-inch heels and enormous silver buckles.

"She's here," he spoke strongly through a pair of thick blackish-purple lips. "Outside."

"Have her come inside."

"She hates music. She won't come inside."

Jobie grumbled as his face scrunched with irritation. The web tattoo condensed with his tightened skin. "No one hates music."

"Apparently she does."

"Is she a Betty?" Jobie pried. "Is she hot?"

Opaque shook his head as he turned to walk away. "Chasing Betties, always chasing the skirts," Opaque caustically mumbled to himself, "Nothing better to do...chasing Betties...writing terrorist manuals..." He casually returned to the blazing heat of the desert.

"Hold this record for me," Jobie demanded the clerk as he removed the headphones. "I'll be back to get it." He continued out the door, following the lead of his younger brother into the dry heat of Arizona.

There, standing next to the curb was the most attractive misfit youth he had ever seen, and it certainly wasn't his brother. His eyes widened and the pace of his heart intensified as he stepped forward to join them. He clutched *The Apolitical Manifesto* with tense fingers as he swaggered up to them in steady cool reserve. He could feel his brother watching him, studying him. He knew that his brother was keen to every thought, every feeling. He always was.

The young girl stood smiling with a postcard perfect expression of bliss and ease. She couldn't have been more than seventeen years of age, though her youth seemed timeless. Jobie felt an immediate and desperate yearning to be a part of her world, her happiness. He had seen so little of it in his life.

"Hello," she greeted him clumsily with a high-pitched voice that mirrored a child's. The pointedness of her cheekbones seemed to almost protrude uncomfortably under her fair skin. Her smile was intoxicating and graciously innocent, like a Catholic schoolgirl. A long and slender nose seemed to offset the proportions of her tiny chin. At an angle, her nostrils seemed enormous. Her over-sized brown corduroy pants concealed any suggestion of legs, though he assumed they were as thin as her gaunt, though pretty horse-like face. A shiny, tight lime-green Adidas T-shirt did show that she needn't wear a bra, and it was clear that she didn't by the way her firm nipples poked under the thin fabric. Her posture was awkward, pigeon-toed with slumped shoulders. The bones of her shoulders and elbows were as sharp as pencils. "Are you Jobie?"

He nodded affirmatively while squinting in the harsh sunlight.

"I'm Treva Rifkin," she announced timidly as she ran her bony fingers through her messy burgundy-colored, shoulder-length hair. She teased her bangs nervously as she giggled. And giggled. She tapped her chest with a stiff finger, giving a visual aid to her introduction. She seemed perfectly incapable of speaking without her hands. Every word was aided and accentuated by elated gestures. "I met Opaque this morning out front of the Bison Witch." She aimed her slender finger down

10

the street, jabbing at the dry air as she closed an eye to focus on the nearby intersection of 4th Avenue.

Jobie shifted his attention briefly to his brother, Rik, or as he obviously preferred, Opaque. Jobie laughed aloud, bringing their conversation to a sudden halt as he humored himself at his brother's expense.

Treva stared at him, calculating his mocking laughter. She didn't like it. There was something vindictive and judgmental about it. She felt it was aimed at her. Anger spontaneously burst inside her skinny body, ignited by his apparent scrutiny. She hated to be laughed at, and she felt hatred toward him for laughing at her. Her large green eyes flared with a neurotic ferocity. Her face suddenly flushed red, speckling her fair skin with an uneven splotchiness. "What are you laughing at?!"

"Nothing," Jobie shrugged with a belligerent and self-gratifying grin, devoid of the knowledge that her mood had completely shifted. "Just...my asshole brother."

She turned to Opaque who nodded politely at her in compliance. She could sense in his compassionate, yet burning red eyes that she had misread the situation. His sensible awareness put her immediately at ease again as if nothing had stirred her. His perceptiveness was clearly a quality lacking in Jobie. "Oh," she mumbled with a belated sigh. Her shoulders slumped forward as her massive eyes twinkled once again. No sooner had her skin discolored, it completely faded back to its smooth delicacy. Her smile followed, revealing a set of awkwardly large teeth. "Your brother tells me you've got something I've been trying to find."

Jobie raised an eye and pursed his lips as he gave a short nod. "Oh really?"

"So I've heard," she told him. "That's what a little birdy told me anyway." Her finger quickly shot toward the tops of the buildings, as if tipping them off to the whereabouts of birds. She raised her bushy brow and batted her long lashes. "Haven't smoked in days."

Jobie glanced down the street, checking for any wandering eyes that may be upon them. He pulled a plastic bag out from his pocket and laid it in her bony hand. "Good stuff," he promised.

She took a quick look at the bag's contents before handing it back to him. "No seeds, no stems..." she mumbled with her sweetly innocent voice that flowered the air around them. She was quite aware of how smitten Jobie was with her. She would play it for all its worth, for all her ego's worth. "Are you a cop?"

His chilling laughter rang loudly through the desert's heat. "A cop? How dare you insult me...if I was a cop I'd have to kill myself."

She let out an awkward and submissive giggle that she quickly stifled by covering her thick lips with a bony hand. There was genuine warmth in her laughter that infected both of them. A silent exchange of smiles followed. "Had to ask. So how much?"

"Forty bucks a quarter."

She looked to the ground, as if seeking the words that rested so comfortably on the end of her tongue. "That's more than I have."

Jobie felt discouraged, even insulted. Had he not found her so attractive, he'd have simply walked away at that moment. "How about thirty-five? Come on, that's a steal. It's worth more."

She gave a relaxed and girlish giggle that again deceived her age. It was one that belonged on a playground. Yet it was her childish demeanor and cutesy little-girl voice that drove Jobie's hormones to the brink of a meltdown. It made him want to conquer her, to chastise her purity with a violent and passionate struggle that she would not win. He wanted that power over her, to destroy the very thing he found so enticing. He felt morbid and twisted for such thoughts. He liked the feeling.

"I'm kind of broke—I only have twenty-five dollars," she confessed. "See, I'm passing through from Colorado—"

"Where you heading?" Jobie interjected.

She shrugged her shoulders. "Beats me."

"We're travelling also," Jobie told her. "We're going to visit every state of the union, before hitting Europe, eventually. We've seen a lot already. In fact, we were in San Diego just yesterday morning. I believe we're going..." He looked to Opaque, who returned the gaze with casual indifference. "We're going to New Orleans. For Mardi Gras."

"Wow! Cool!" she exclaimed excitedly. "Can I go too?"

Jobie's eyes lit up, as she expected.

"February," Opaque muttered with a firm and commanding voice. "Mardi Gras isn't until February."

"Oh," Treva sighed. "That's too bad..."

"Well, let's just take the scenic route," Jobie suggested.

Treva looked at him, at the spider's web tattoo spanning his hollow cheeks, at his messy hair with the cheap dye job. She studied his powerfully hypnotic eyes that squinted in the heat of the desert. They seemed to be undressing her, violating her. The thought made her smile. He was exactly the kind of guy that her father would despise. "All right," she declared with excitement. "Let's find a ride."

MONDAY, SEPTEMBER 7, 1998

Outskirts of Kyle, Texas
10:47pm

"This is it," Cindy Dunne resolved. "This conversation will be our last."

Tamika Tovar fell silent, writhing in discomfort as she clutched the phone against her ear. She didn't want this, but she seemed to never get what she wanted from life. Misery seemed part of its endurance, with death the only release. These thoughts had been the source of many intimate conversations she had shared with Cindy, but as the final hour approached, it all seemed very irrational. She didn't want this, she never did.

"Tamika, you're not talking to me," Cindy complained. "Are you still there?"

"I'm here." Tamika pulled the black sheets up to her thick neck. She felt somewhat more at ease, simply knowing that her obese body was covered from view, despite her solitude.

The heat of the night penetrated the boxy trailer. Black tapestries hung from the walls of her room. White and red candles dripped over ornate iron fixtures secured to the thin wall. The room was otherwise dark. *The Taste of Cindy* by The Jesus And Mary Chain played softly from a nearby cassette player. It was a significant song, it was their song. The seventh on the *Psychocandy* album, it took nearly half the tape to find the courage to give that first kiss. But that was years ago, long before the tumultuous ride that their relationship had become. Cindy's violent mood swings and erratic panic attacks seemed to always keep happiness beyond their reach. At seventeen years of age, Cindy decided she had had enough of life. As the only love of her life, Tamika agreed on a similar fate. She always told her that she would give her life for the love she felt. Now the clock ticked...

"Soon I'll know the answer to the big question," Cindy marveled optimistically. "Where we go from here. Do you think we'll meet, or do you think the lights will just go out?"

"I don't feel well," Tamika said solemnly.

Cindy laughed. "Oh, listen to you! Like it's going to matter. We'll both be dead soon. What difference does it make?"

"None?"

"Right, none," Cindy insisted. She had expected Tamika's hesitance. She knew that Tamika never followed through with anything she ever promised. Her poor self-esteem was always

15

the overbearing deterent to all her endeavors. No, Tamika wouldn't do it, and they both knew this. Likewise, both were aware that this was their final conversation. Cindy didn't share Tamika's passive nature. Cindy's word was her honor, despite how infrequently she gave it. "Tamika...thank you for being my friend."

Tamika sat perfectly still, numbed by the words. It was the closest Cindy had ever come to telling her that she loved her.

"I've got to go," Cindy's voice trembled awkwardly. Her anger quickly surfaced, ignited by her inability to control her emotions. "Fuck it..." She slammed the phone down violently. These were the last words ever spoken between them.

In the morning, before the sun surfaced, Tamika crawled out of bed. She hadn't slept. Her round face was puffy from all the tears she'd shed the night before. Her kinky curly black hair was a frightful mess, as always. She grabbed the length of it with both hands, twisting two pigtails together behind each ear, tying her hair with thin red satin ribbons. She slipped a long flowing black velvet gown over her shoulders as she gazed dully out the window. The sirens hadn't come yet, but it didn't surprise her. Knowing Cindy's parents, it would take them days to find her body in the camper on the front lawn—her bedroom. And knowing them, there'd be a party later that night.

She stumbled over to her dresser, removing all her favorite outfits, which didn't amount to much. She crammed them inside an empty pillowcase, stuffing her small collection of cassette tapes with it. She diverted her attention in the dim light to the plastic baby doll on the nightstand. It was the only thing Cindy ever gave to her, something she found alongside the road one drunken night. She tucked the doll inside the pillowcase and left the room.

Darkness filled the confines of the tiny run-down trailer, but she knew her way quite well. This had been home her entire life. As she passed through the living room, her large brown eyes squinted at the sight of the snowy static on the television set. Her mother was passed out on the couch, still clutching a glass of tequila that she had partially spilt on herself. The ashtray was full of butts from the night before. She had a visitor, it was clear, but there was nothing new with that. Her mother based her identity on the men she acquired. Tamika was quite aware of her reputation throughout the trailer park. Anyone needing a good time knew where to go. Her mother claimed that it was in her Hispanic blood to be so sexually active. Tamika never understood why she didn't share the same affliction, unless the African-American blood of her father's stifled her *Hispanic fire*.

She crept through the living room to the front door. On the plywood display next to the door was a photograph of herself, taken at Christmas many years earlier. The child in the picture was coming out of her skin with excitement, clutching a wrapped package with tiny fingers. Her expression was almost constipated with excitement—her lips were stretched into a long, thin horizontal line. The process of taking the picture had clearly delayed the opening of the gift, therefore perfectly capturing her impatient enthusiasm. The photograph had always haunted her—that child had died long ago. She removed the photograph from the shelf and stuffed it into her pillowcase. She took one last look at her mother before leaving.

"Thanks for nothing, bitch," she mumbled as she left, never to return again.

The air was already warm and the sky was beginning to glow a pale blue. The sun would be up soon.

As she stumbled up the gravel road in the quiet darkness, she thought it interesting how strangely inhibited she felt. There were no eyes watching her, yet she felt grossly analyzed. She felt repulsive and disgusting, fat and ugly. She figured her poor appearance was based on the amount of food she ate. Well, she wouldn't have to worry about that. She wasn't sure exactly where she was going, but she knew wherever it was, food would be scarce. She liked the idea. She finally smiled, stumbling to the top of the hill where the lights of all the trailers scattered the horizon, as far as she could see. This was hell, she estimated as she continued to the main light source, the nearby Diamond Shamrock gas station. The sky was coming alive, transforming from blue to deep purple and orange.

She wondered if Cindy's spirit was following her. She hoped as much. She knew that Cindy would take care of her. Cindy was the only person who ever did.

By the time she had arrived at the gas station, the sun was already peaking on the horizon. Old pick-up trucks with full loads idled before every pump, readying for a day of hard labor. She stumbled into the harsh fluorescent lights, feeling absolute discomfort in her obese body. She spotted a familiar man pumping gas, a man she found passed out on her mother from time to time. She was amazed that she could even remember all those men, all those faces. He looked at her as she approached, squinting while rearranging his chew with his tongue.

"Shouldn't you be on your way to school, young lady?" he asked her with a distinct Texas twang.

"I need a ride," she told him.

"I didn't figure you were going to school, not with that bag over your shoulder. Where you heading?"

"Where you heading?"

"San Antonio."

"Sounds good to me," she said. "Can I get a lift?"

"What you got to offer me?" he asked.

She looked to the ground nervously, then raised her head sheepishly. "Nothing."

"Gas, grass, or ass, sweetheart," he recited from memory, impressed by his own cleverness. "No free rides in this world."

"No thanks, then," she told him as she continued to the station, toward the blinding white lights. She eyed all the backward country folk walking in and out of the small store. It was a pleasant reminder of why she felt such a need to leave. She didn't belong. She didn't really belong anywhere, but she knew that this was definitely not the place for her.

"Darlin'," a woman's voice shot from a nearby pump. "If you're needing a ride somewhere, I could take you to Austin. I work downtown. State Capitol building."

Tamika smiled, overwhelmed with relief. "Thank you."

The woman lit another cigarette while fluffing her enormous bangs into place. The signs were clearly marked *No Smoking*. "Why you leaving?" she asked Tamika as they stood outside her primer-colored Ford Escort.

"Look around you," Tamika said.

The woman laughed. "Climb inside, it's unlocked."

The journey to Austin was rather quick, aided by the comfort of silence. The construction along Interstate 35 was a good distraction, though it slowed traffic to a near halt. They listened quietly to the morning program on KVET.

"This city is growing too fast," the woman said as she lit up another cigarette. "No place I'd want to live. In ten years this city will be enormous, like Houston."

Tamika smiled briefly as though she had any interest at all.

"It's a hard world, darlin'," the woman told her between drags as they slowly progressed through the morning's traffic. "Ain't nothing comes easy."

Tamika nodded timidly.

"There's a place in town you may want to check out," the woman continued. "Find a lot of kids that wear the same kind of dark clothes you do. There on the Drag. Ever been on the Drag?"

Tamika gave another passive nod.

"I think you should spend some time down there, get a feel for the world before you take off too far. You may find that you'd be better off where you were. Anyway, I can take you down there, but you're on your own, then. I'm sorry. I wish I could help more."

"Thank you," Tamika told her kindly before they fell into silence again. She didn't speak another word until she was dropped off in front of the Church of Scientology on Guadalupe. "Please don't mention this to anyone."

The woman smiled. "You're safe with me. Now take good care of yourself."

Tamika thanked her once again before slamming the door.

Guadalupe Street was vibrantly alive with young students rushing to their morning classes. The businesses were already open, serving breakfast and coffee to the tired faces whom worked the real world. The street smelled of grime, much like a real city. She liked the smell. A group of young disheveled kids were splayed on the corner in front of the Bagel Shop. They were sound asleep like a pile of dirty dogs—all but one that stared at her with fiery red eyes. The stranger's eyes locked onto her—eyes that were surrounded by a vicious war-paint of cheap cosmetics. A burnt orange and black frightwig rose above the person's head like the feathers of an Indian's headdress. Then he smiled at her, his black lips curving into the most natural expression she had ever seen. She returned the gesture comfortably as she wandered closer. He sat up and studied her as she stood over the sleeping mound of dirty youths.

"Hello," she whispered to him. She realized he was quite young, yet strangely intuitive in his observations. "I'm Tamika Tovar."

He bowed his head gracefully. "Opaque," he introduced himself with an unexpectedly strong voice. "Have a seat. Join us."

Friday, September 11, 1998

Austin, Texas
10:33pm

The rain dripped down the tall pane windows of the Palmer Auditorium, smearing the lights of the city to the rhythms of the Austin Symphony. Soft lights caressed the stage with delicate layers of pastels. Behind the musicians was a banner listing all the corporate sponsors of the event, *The Third Annual Swing Symphony*. Judging by the immensity of the audience, the symphony fund-raiser was a success.

Professor Vaughn Richter leaned back in his chair as he studied every movement of the conductor's baton, yet he witnessed nothing. It was all felt deep within where dreams and passions materialize. He thought back to a time early in his life when the seeds of his inspiration were sown. His recollections were vivid, he could almost feel the breeze blowing through the rusty screen, whipping the caramel colored curtain in slow swirls. His father sat at his desk, reading one book while holding his place in another. His back was turned to him, much as it always was. He knew this part of his father quite well, but his eyes were shrouded in mystery. In fact, he had no recollection of what color they even were. From a nearby radio, the music of Hoagy Carmichael filled the air with tones as rich as the fragrance of wildflowers. It was the first time he really remembered the impact of music, how it controlled his heart and steered his emotions. That very moment seemed somehow orchestrated by the music that solidified his past, secured in memory like a velvet bookmark. His love began from that moment on, both in music and in his determination to be the great man he considered his father to be.

Generous applause showered the conductor as Gershwin's *Nice Work If You Can Get It* came to a close. The rain slammed mercilessly against the massive green domed roof. The conductor took an appreciative bow before turning his baton to the orchestra.

As a devout enthusiast of the genre, Vaughn could attend a performance like this every night of his life. In an age so far removed from class and elegance, an event such as this sadly came but once a year.

He was rather disappointed that the program contained not a single work from his favorite composition team, Rodgers and Hart. Their unlikely union defined the humble lives of a lost

21

era's working class. They were the perfect combination, with Richard Rodgers' flawlessly crafted music supplying the foundation for the most sincere and thoughtful lyrics ever penned to song. Lorenz Hart was a poetic genius, a man whose words melded to the core of the human soul.

Across the circular table, he could feel the eyes of Doctor Schtepp. He needn't look to know they were upon him. He could feel their presence, trying desperately to penetrate his psyche, to force an insight into his sacred identity. Schtepp was the perfect colleague—determined, intelligent, comprehensively researched, and highly educated. He had a strong work ethic that perfectly matched his own. Otherwise, there was little more to be said. He believed that if you hadn't a good thing to say, there was no use for words. On a non-professional level, he kept his silence in regard to Doctor Schtepp.

Sitting next to his colleague was Virginia Jahnke, the development director of the Austin Civic Opera. She was an attractive woman, despite her slight obesity. The beauty of her face was somehow reliant upon its fullness. He couldn't imagine her appearance any other way. She was sophisticated and savvy, with a flair for style and a genuine artistry with cosmetics. She seemingly had a weakness for Schtepp, which Vaughn assumed was based on his pathetic nature. He was a man with money and little more. Her kindness to him, he believed went no further than the hopes of his generosity toward the Opera. She seldom spoke with Vaughn, considering him either too modest or too frugal to become a notable donor to the arts.

As the conductor delivered his stale and over-rehearsed humor to the warmly receptive crowd, Vaughn was reminded of the ceremony for his undergraduate degree many decades ago. Same tacked-on charm, same rhetoric. He clearly recalled the feeling of that stuffy auditorium, enduring the words that parted him from the reason for his attendance. Unlike those times, his personal research projects had intensified in public value beyond the chemical formula for lysergic acid diethylamide. His life, as he had always dreamed, finally would make a difference on mankind. His father would have been proud.

He glanced at the program once again to see that it was the last song of the night, Cole Porter's *Begin the Beguine*. It was one of his all-time favorites. He pondered the cumulative worth of the memories that defined his life, and how this song seemed to somehow thread itself throughout. As the music stirred life into the still atmosphere, Vaughn leaned forward and smiled. It was almost as if he could reach out and touch the fogged windows of his father's Chrysler Imperial. That is where the song took him. The summer of 1966, a night he would not forget. It was that very night that he resolved this song to be his favorite, as it played softly over the radio—his only contact with the outside world. The image of the twisted oak trees swaying in the cool breeze stood erect in memory like a statue of honor bearing his name. Outside the car, the crescent moon shined on a vast and empty countryside road, with every shimmering star visible in the blackened sky. In the expansive backseat of the car, alone and far from civilization, Lenora Craig was losing her virginity. And so was he.

He raised the wineglass to his lips, sipping the smooth pinot noir as he watched the bows of the violins move in one great, synchronized motion. The moment he received his Masters degree, the moment he accepted his life's career as a chemistry professor at the University of Texas—all chained together by the memory of this one song.

He glanced across the table at the other faces who shared his space. He could see in their eyes that his exuberance was not shared. Doctor Schtepp was far away in thought, as usual— probably scheming ways of spending more time with him. Virginia Jahnke smiled, as she always did. Her eyes studied the occupants of a nearby table—the board of directors for the Vi-Tel software corporation. Otherwise, she was completely oblivious to the fact that timeless romantic music played, calling upon her own spent youth. So far was it lost from her that she failed to even recognize its voice harkening through the rhythms like the ghost of a childhood friend. It was a game to them all. A fashion show, of sorts. The music was there only for ambiance, for its role in the prestige they sought to obtain. Few noticed, and even fewer cared. Vaughn cared, he cared a great deal in both regards—not just for the wonderful music, but also for the prominence that he would soon acquire. In just one year, everything in his life would be quite different.

When the music left the auditorium, the people followed, shuffling themselves slowly into the lobby with impersonal smiles.

"Would you care to join me for a drink?" Schtepp asked Vaughn as they stood by the doors in the lobby. The rain trickled down the glass, bleeding the outside world of all its color. "Maybe at the Elephant Room?"

"Oh...not tonight, I'm afraid," Richter responded politely with a firm and deeply rich voice. His vocal cords would've suited an opera singer. The strength of his voice was amplified by the determination that illuminated from his deep-set eyes. "It's been a long day."

23

Schtepp nodded defeatedly as he adjusted the hair that rested over his bald crown. He looked up at Vaughn's face, atop his tall muscular frame. He found himself drowning in his eyes. He felt himself lose his own identity briefly as he floundered to escape the comfort of his comrade's towering confidence. Yet, there was nothing he wanted more than that loss.

"Did you enjoy the show?" Vaughn asked calmly.

"Yes, yes I did," he replied as he scooted closer to the front door. He held it open for Vaughn, watching as he glided through it with the stature of royalty. Once outside, Schtepp opened his black umbrella and turned to Vaughn, staring at his perfectly sculpted face, his handsomely male features, and the gray beard that gave his pronounced jaw a sublime dignity. He could tell by his thick and dark eyebrows that his short gray hair had once been the same dark shade. Together they stood under the umbrella as the rain formed an arc around them. It covered them like a webbed claw. Schtepp looked up at him and nodded. "Well, have a good night."

Vaughn smiled politely as he pulled his emerald-colored jacket closed. He looked at his watch, realizing that it was already eleven-fifteen, much later than he had anticipated. When he glanced back up, lightning ripped across the sky, followed immediately by a deafening thunder. "We'll talk again on Monday." He turned away and walked briskly through the parking lot as the cold rain streamed down upon him like confetti.

11:01pm

"Thunder freaks me out," Tamika confessed as the rain streamed over the Bagel Shop's green awning. She was crouched in the corner of the deck, safely tucked away in the shadows. She cradled her legs in her arms to conceal her weight. Her pillowcase sat nearby, safely dry under a wooden table. The plastic head of the doll peeped from within, floating in a pool of dark clothing. "I hope it stops soon."

Jobie stretched his dirty hand outside of the deck, reaching into the cold water that descended from the colorless sky. He inhaled deeply, breathing in the grimy stench of the city that intensified with the rain. It smelled of an aged society, used like a whore. "I can't see this rain lasting long. I don't think it ever rains this much here in Texas." It didn't even occur to him that Tamika would know. In fact, he was hardly aware of her presence. To him, it was just Treva along with two other spectators. He leaned back against the wall and propped his bare feet up on one of the wooden tables. "We're not staying in this town very long."

Inside the bakery, it was completely dark, closed for the night. Quiet, as was the rest of the Drag.

"How did you guys get all the way to Texas?" Tamika asked. She hoped her questions would bring her closer to their tight circle. She felt like an outsider, unsure of the club's secret handshake. She looked over to Treva and smiled. In her she saw a potential companion, if for no other reason than the fact that she found her to be prettier than herself.

Treva sat on the floor in demure posture, rolling a fat joint as she sipped from a Diet Coke. A cigarette burned slowly, hanging from her mouth, quenching her appetite. "We couldn't find a ride." Her cheerful voice trembled like a feeble child. She licked the edge of the fine paper, finishing the joint that would relinquish Jobie's once impressive supply. She glanced at Tamika, thinking that she could see the two of them becoming closer. If for no other reason than the fact that she knew she was prettier than Tamika. "We found a freight train eventually." She reverted her attention back to matters at hand, the lighting of her joint. A dead silence followed.

"How about a game of truth or dare?" Jobie suggested, bored with their trite discussion. His question was clearly aimed at Treva, hoping to pry vital information pertaining to her morals.

She hadn't even noticed him speaking. She was too preoccupied trying to light the joint with her cigarette. Her face was scrunchy and focused with one eye closed and a cocked brow. He waited until she had it lit before rephrasing the question to be more direct. "How old were you when you first had sex, Treva?"

She took a hit off the joint before passing it over to him. She let out a deep cough before taking a drag off her cigarette. As she released the smoke into the sticky air, she smiled diffidently. "I was pretty young, and to be honest, I'd really rather not say." She turned to Opaque, raising her brow to post the same question.

Opaque was centered on top of the middle table with a black comforter shrouding his thin body. He towered over them like an effigy. He shifted his silent attention to her, feeling her thoughts, studying her feelings. His enormous military bag sat at his side, overflowing with all of his expensive and eccentric clothing. He returned her gaze with confidence, masking his thoughts behind ghoulish make-up and a hollow expression. He kept his emotions well tempered, though his opinion of her was souring by the day. He honestly wished he had never introduced her to Jobie. He had been the third wheel ever since. "I'm not into sex, and I'm not one to tell. Tamika?"

Tamika's eyes widened as the question came to her. The honest answer wasn't an easy one. Not for her ego. She'd have happily given away her virginity years ago, had someone wished to take it. There were many boys with whom she would've shared the experience, but the feeling was never reciprocated. She still harbored bitterness about it, and now that the years had passed, she felt she had somehow missed the boat. She couldn't turn back time, and there wasn't any girl her age that she knew who hadn't already lost her virginity to a man. Even her friend Cindy would occasionally have sex with a much older man, a fact that caused an unbearable rift in their trust. It not only derailed Tamika's confidence, but also made her green with envy. Her chastity invariably became a conviction, a cover from the difficult truth she kept close to herself. "I'm a lesbian," she told them proudly. "I have no interest in men. My first experience was with my friend Cindy *years* ago, like maybe when I was fourteen."

Jobie nodded his head casually as though he cared. His lungs were still filled with smoke as he passed the joint back to Treva. "Don't bogart the fucker, Treva," he requested, knowing that she had practically consumed his entire bag on her own. He turned to Tamika, who stared with those frail, puppy dog eyes. Her low self-esteem annoyed the hell out of him. "I was fourteen also."

"How did you get your nickname, Opaque?" Tamika asked timidly.

"I made it up."

"I used to have a nickname," Treva exclaimed between hits as her arms suddenly exploded into the misty wet air. Her fingers wiggled with excitement. "My mother always called me Purty. Isn't that ridiculous?"

Everyone laughed, mostly at her ostentatious behavior. Jobie's quiet comment went undetected under the cackling laughter. "Fitting."

"I always liked my mother," Treva said as she passed the joint over to Jobie before taking a quick gulp from the Diet Coke. Her high-pitched, childish voice absorbed the entire focus of their attention. "My father..." She shook her head slowly before she continued, "what a dick."

"Why don't you like music?" Jobie asked her out of nowhere. "How can anyone not like music?"

"My family *loves* music. In fact, believe it or not, my grandmother was once in a band! Way back in the fifties, they were called Strawberry and the Milkshakes. She was Strawberry, because of her hair. Just like mine. My grandmother was a wacko. A different kind of crazy than my dad...I fucking *hate* that asshole. *Hate him.*"

Opaque watched intently as the anger burst inside her. He had seen it several times before. Her brow furrowed and her teeth grated while she studied the ground, locked into a memory. He imagined the scenes that played out in her mind, the horrors of her past that she struggled to contain in a locked box. The anger took ownership of her, enflaming her body with a coarse ruddiness of dappling hives. Her skin discolored slightly as if lava from an internal volcano seeped from her pores. It spread quickly, flowing down her arms to her bony fingers. Her expression was lethal and venomous. For a fleeting second, she almost appeared monstrous—then suddenly her innocent smile reappeared, extinguishing the negativity altogether with one quick breath. Her tense, splotchy complexion dispersed as well, residing below the surface of her skin, waiting for the next manic tremor.

"Yeah...my father," Treva said as she examined her arm, scratching it nervously to quench the hives spawned by her own neurosis, "he *loved* music."

Jobie passed the joint back to her. He hadn't noticed a thing. "What's the wildest thing you've ever done sexually?"

She smiled innocuously as she took a quick hit from the small roach poised between her thin fingers. Jobie smiled briefly as well, waiting to reveal his amazing exploits, like the time he made out with two drunk girls after a punk show.

"I swear," Treva began, "I was always interested in sex, even at a young age. I knew men wanted it, and I knew they wanted me. I remember when I was in fifth grade I used to meet with a group of boys in the alley after school. They'd skip lunch so that they could give me their lunch money to see me naked." She took the last hit off the roach before flicking it into the rain. "Soon the small group became half my class! I was a celebrity!"

Jobie glanced down at his kilt, checking to see if his erection was obvious. It wasn't. If he had a dime to his name, he'd have offered a trip to the back alley, just like the old days for her...

"I got really good at reading men," Treva admitted. "I remember being in a mall once at about the same age, and I could tell which ones would, and which ones wouldn't—all from a look in their eyes."

"How do you know you were right?" Tamika asked.

"Experience. Besides, I've seen that look my whole life. I know it when I see it." She peered into Jobie's striking eyes, reaffirming her statement. She smiled for a brief moment before she continued. "I didn't even need birth control back then—I had never even had a period! I remember fantasizing about telling my dad that I was pregnant at that age. I really wish I would've been. His response would've made it all worth it. Sex is such a powerful thing."

"Who showed you that power?" Opaque asked, following the lead of suspicion.

She avoided the question, hiding behind a phony facsimile of a grin.

Jobie raised his eyebrows as his heart rate quickly increased. Treva could sense this, she didn't even need to look at him to know. His interest in her seemed to seep from his pores.

"I wanted to be good at sex. I was determined to be the perfect lay." She paused to sip from her soda as her small audience waited in uncomfortable silence. "One Christmas...I believe I was in seventh grade at the time, I tried an experiment with my father's best friend. He was an annoying prick. Always on the go with the church, talking down to people that didn't share his beliefs. I fucked him senseless...I wanted so badly to have his child so my father could never forget. Didn't happen. I saw him again the following year at a family camping trip. My father packed the camcorder for whatever reason...I hid it in my tent under some clothes and left it running. It was at the perfect angle, though the lighting wasn't very great. As I expected, he came to my tent for a visit in the middle of the night. Caught the whole act on film! I sent him a copy a month later. He offered to pay me five hundred dollars to destroy it. I declined. I doubt he regrets anything more in his life. I wish I still had it. Unfortunately, I left it for my father to find after I ran away."

Everyone rearranged themselves from awkward discomfort as the rain trickled from the awning, splattering against the filthy sidewalk.

"This may sound like an odd question," Tamika offered obliquely, "but have you ever had an orgasm?"

"Hmm..." Treva contemplated as she took a quick sip from her Diet Coke. "I'm not sure. I suppose not." She shrugged her shoulders as she lit another cigarette. The question seemed irrelevant to her train of thought. "You know," she continued, "whenever someone pissed me off, I always found a way through sex to get even, usually ten-fold. For instance, I had a classmate whom I hated. She was one of those annoying popular bitches everyone wanted to fuck. I hate girls like that. She had heard from a friend that the football team had pulled a train on me— which was only partially true. Two players, and I only did it to keep up my reputation at the time. Anyway, she insulted me in

front of some of my friends. She called me a whore to my face,
the stupid bitch. I wanted to kill her. That weekend, I went out
of my way to score one of the players that I hadn't yet—her
boyfriend. I found out afterward that I had actually taken his
virginity. Word about it got out, thanks to my big mouth, and
they broke up."

Tamika leaned forward uncomfortably to check the clock
inside the bakery just as lightning ripped across the sky, trailed
by bellowing thunder. "It's eleven-fifteen."

"So what about you, Jobie?" Treva asked with her sweetly
juvenile voice. "What's the wildest thing you've done sexually?"

Jobie leaned back, placing his hands behind his head. "I'm
not the type to kiss and tell."

Saturday, September 12, 1998

1:16pm

Treva strolled carelessly down the Drag as a sparse rain trickled from the misty gray sky. She swung a can of Diet Coke in her claw-like hand as a cigarette dangled from her smiling lips. The rain dampened her dirty scalp, pasting her raspberry-colored hair to her prominent cheekbones and fair skin. Her wet shirt clung to her bony ribcage, accenting the perkiness of her hard nipples under the thin lime-green fabric.

Her cheery disposition shined amongst the dour faces shielded beneath colorful umbrellas. Women gave passing glances of discontent like drenched kittens, mortified that their cosmetic allure had washed away with the rain. The men, on the other hand, secretly ravaged her body with their sordid imaginations. Their lascivious attention fertilized her ego, building upon her personal identity of objectified beauty. She held their gaze, flirting shamelessly with bedtime eyes that beckoned decadently sinful pleasures. It had been months since she had allowed a man custody of her body. She humored the idea of luring one or two young students to the alley where they could have their way before leaving her naked and neglected, discarded like trash. The thought brought a smile to her meager face.

"Spare some change?" a young girl asked from underneath the Eckerd awning.

Treva stopped in mid-stride as she placed her wrists to her scrawny hips. Her posture spoke sassiness. "You're asking *me* for money?" She pointed to the pavement with a stiff finger before dramatically poking at her own flat chest. "You're loungin' in *my* bedroom!" Her tiny giggle reduced her confrontational manner. It screamed of innocence. She raised her shoulders with heavy exasperation as she rolled her eyes dramatically. "Whatever..." She strutted back down the sidewalk with a meandering liquid-like motion, haphazard and carefree.

Her gaze fell to the concrete that collected pools of water in its broken surface. Several layers of cement comprised the sidewalk in its entirety, each from a variance of construction throughout past decades. The result was a patchwork of dissimilar grays that unified into a solid singular surface, an olla-podrida of design.

There came a rift in the flow of pedestrian traffic as she approached 22nd. A dark male presence stood in her path with crossed arms and a daunting scowl. He raised his eyebrows salaciously at the sight of her, allowing his forehead to crinkle unnaturally over acne scars. He was tall and muscular with menacing, angry eyes. His attire was black, including his back-turned baseball cap that concealed his greasy orange hair.

"Who are you?" he hissed at her. His voice was shrill, a near caterwaul.

Treva smiled comfortably as she sucked the final drag from her cigarette, flicking the butt of it into a stream of water that raced toward a nearby gutter. "Why?"

His expression hardened like block ice. "Because I asked."

"My name is Treva," she resigned with her silly sweet voice. "I just came to town. And your name?"

His eyes rolled with sheer disappointment. His lips pursed like a sphincter. "You don't know?"

She raised her hands into the moist air while shaking her head emphatically. "I don't know...sorry."

"You need to know who I am," he told her flatly. "I'm Dickhead." He looked to gauge her response. "Got it?"

She nodded, though she didn't get it at all.

"See all these people around here on the corner?" he asked her, gesturing to a gregarious bunch of filthy kids loitering in front of the Bagel Shop. "Ask them about me, they'll tell you."

"Hmm...I'd rather you tell me. What is there to know?"

He smiled proudly, revealing his chipped and stained teeth. "Let's go have a seat." His voice was as enticing as grating metal.

She followed him to the arcade where they sat on the dry walkway alongside the inner wall of the Scientology building. She took a quick sip of her Diet Coke and faced him directly.

He raised his voice to a steady monotone. "What do you want to know?"

"Obviously what you want me to know," she replied with contrasting vivaciousness. She could see in his indignant eyes that he'd rather she hear from someone else, just to add to his mystique and validity. She could tell that she wasn't playing along very well. "Come on, tell me about it."

"Well..." he began slowly as he forced himself into a relaxed pose against the crumbling white wall, "I came from Atlanta, I've been here around a year, maybe longer."

She nodded supportively.

"When I got here, a lot of the businesses were coming down on us because of the Oogles, and there was a lot of tension out here. Shops would give us shit, the cops were starting to enforce the *no-camping* laws to keep us off the streets. I don't know how it all came down, but it's kind of history down here anymore...one night a group of about half a dozen Straight

Edgers came to the Drag and started bustin' people up. They don't like us."

"What is that?" Treva asked anxiously, pleasantly enthralled in the direction of his story. "Is that a gang?"

"Kind of," he told her. "Straight Edge, the vegetarian assholes who live some puritan lifestyle...they're as much a gang as skinheads are, but they just don't drink like the skinheads."

She nodded as if she knew anything about what he was telling her. All that mattered to her was the word *gang*. She always fancied the thug lifestyle.

"Some of my friends ended up in the hospital, it was bad. Really bad. As the legend goes, I organized a couple of the tougher Crusties, we had about four of us, and we stayed on guard each night until they returned. They never did, but from that moment on, anytime we ever got shit from anyone, my boys would keep the peace for us out here. When the stores would give us trouble, I'd bust out their windows after hours. The cops would talk to us, but no one knew any different, they had no proof...so we started getting more respect. Do you get what I'm saying?"

Treva nodded. "Have you seen the other gang since then?"

"Nah," he shrugged half-heartedly.

"So who all is part of your gang?" she asked.

"We're not a gang," he decided. "We're generally pacifists. Just don't fuck with us."

"What is a Crusty? And what is an Oogle?"

"Crusties are the real thing. We live on the streets, we move from city to city—it's a lifestyle. Oogles are posers. They're kids from the suburbs pretending to be street. Mommy brings them money and picks them up when it rains. Like I said, posers."

"Have you been a Crusty very long?"

"Long enough," he replied defensively. "I was part of the Five Points crew in Atlanta. I was in Athens, Asheville, Philly...I spent some time with the spider punks in New York."

She almost didn't want to ask, fearing that her redundant inquiries would diminish her own street credibility. It was clear that the word punk seemed synonymous with renegade. "What's a spider punk?"

"They live in the trees, they sleep in hammocks way in the tops, no one knows they're there. They live in Central Park."

"I think Jobie is a Crusty punk, then," Treva mumbled aloud, speaking her random thoughts for no apparent reason. "But he doesn't sleep in trees."

"Boyfriend?" His fists clenched briefly.

"Not really." Her mind quickly went from Jobie to his empty bag of pot. She could use a new hook-up. "Do you smoke?" she asked under her breath with a coy and playful smile.

He grinned pompously. It almost seemed like a taxing effort for him. "Looking to get high?"

She nodded her head quickly, excitedly. "Do you know anybody?"

"I know a lot of people," he boasted.

"Can you get acid?" she whispered with bright enthusiasm.

He smiled confidently, though his eyes were still tense and bitter. He casually reached inside the pockets of his black jeans and unfolded a flier. "Skin Ensemble show tonight...remember this name, and you can tell Talon that Dickhead sent you, he owes me a big favor..."

1:17pm

Tamika glanced over her shoulder, out the Metro coffee shop's second-story window overlooking the Drag. The window's glass was streaked from the rain that was in a current state of submission. On the street below, the traffic scooted slowly in opposing directions, clogged and congested. The windshield wipers of each car alternated to a different rhythm, scraping across dry glass as if anticipating another shower at any second.

She rearranged herself in the hard metal chair that was shaped like a box with harsh right angles. The backrest was made of separated metal, making tiny waffle patterns on her elbows and arms. She leaned forward on the glass tabletop, admiring the blue shadowing of Opaque's cheeks. His face was flushed white, his lips a blackish-purple, his cheeks shadowed with a misty dark midnight blue that somehow blended up to the circumference of his smoldering red eyes. His color scheme was almost patriotic.

Over the metal guardrail, she could hear the occupants of the coffee shop laughing happily as the music of Clan of Xymox's album *Medusa* played over the speakers. She wished they would go away.

In the distance she could see the black metal tread-plate stairs that separated the two floors. The bottom floor was softly lit by rows of track lighting that reflected dully off the polished cement. Upstairs felt like an attic, with the entire shop being

34

nothing more than a modified warehouse. The brick walls were the color of ash.

"We're not staying in Austin long," Opaque told her flatly as he slowly stirred his café mocha. His arms were completely lost inside elbow-length, black satin opera gloves. They hugged his pale skin tightly. Silver claws like those of a buzzard extended from his fingers, clicking against the ceramic mug to the lethargic rhythm of the music. "We'll be leaving here soon."

"Where are you going?" she asked.

"Everywhere." He took a dainty sip of his simmering drink as his eyes followed the perimeter of the glass tabletop. Its shape reminded him of an amoeba. "Heading east to New Orleans."

"Sounds exciting."

"I'm excited to go," he told her. "Hopefully our luck won't change for the worse."

She glanced up at a young couple, both doused in heavy black garb. She glared with envy at the young girl's thin shapely body before returning her attention to Opaque. He was watching her. In his eyes it was clear that he had seen right through her thoughts. She could see the judgement in his eyes, though she didn't fear the verdict. He was merely observing and understanding who she was. Apparently understanding too well. "What made you want to leave home?" she asked him.

His eyes squinted and his mouth tensed as though he had swallowed his tongue. "Had to."

"Why?"

"Our family had trouble," he admitted. "It was always Jobie. He and my dad had some problems. I never understood why, and if there was a reason, I never knew. My dad drank too much, and then there'd be some problems...it was sometime in the spring, possibly April...I remember that the night was chilly and there was a terrible wind. It really seemed like it was going to rain, I remember it well. It never did, though." He sat quietly a moment. "Such a strange memory, but it's the tree that I remember the most. Funny...the tree was being blown really hard, the branches were banging against the house...the sound of the wind drowned out the screams coming from the other room. I opened the window, I was scared. I was always scared. Scared that dad would come after me next. I climbed out onto the roof and to the largest branch, hiding in the tree as I had since I was a little kid."

Tamika watched him, seizing the discomfort that he felt by reaching out and grabbing his hand. It was tight and rigid.

"I clung to the branch, and the wind was whipping the whole tree, I felt as if the entire world shook with instability. I could see inside Jobie's room, I watched dad beat him. I had never seen it before, and I will never forget it. When dad left to go downstairs, I climbed onto the roof and knocked on Jobie's window. I watched him cry...I had never seen that before. My image of him shattered, and I liked what stood in place—he was scared, just like me. I climbed inside the window and he told me dad was coming back, that I had to leave. I asked what happened. He wouldn't say. I could feel the wind pushing me around as I watched him lay in a curled ball on the floor. His lips were bloody. I asked him to get up, to go. I didn't have any idea what I was saying." He took a sip of his smoldering drink and stared into the dark liquid.

"Did he get up?" Tamika asked.

"He asked where we'd go, and it was clear he wasn't sold on my idea. Honestly, I wasn't either. I suggested Portland since he had a friend there. He visited regularly, doing research for his book at the Liberation Collective on weekends...he got up, and he was obviously in pain, holding his gut, limping to the window. My heart was racing, I was so scared, everything was chaos. Dad would come up soon, we had to leave, we had only a few minutes. I stumbled across the roof and back into my room, filling a military bag with all my clothes and keepsakes. Then came the sound of dad's footsteps, slowly, drunken...up the stairs again. They were angry belligerent steps."

Tamika stared with wide eyes that begged him to continue.

"I tossed the bag out the window so that it rolled onto the lawn below. I helped Jobie climb out his window, he was in a lot of pain. Dad could've killed him, and maybe he would've. I put my arm around him and helped him to the tree, pushing him up into it as dad opened the window and screamed at us. He was violently angry, but too drunk to follow us. I stood there staring at him, consumed with fear and humility and an enormous feeling of failure to him as Jobie climbed down the tree. Dad was disappointed with me, I could see it in his eyes. I began to second-guess my motivations, then I thought of Jobie. I had to leave, I had to get him out of there. I knew dad would follow, he'd go downstairs and out the front door just in time to catch Jobie and beat his ass. But he didn't. He just stared at me, hurt. His eyes said everything, he needn't speak. We looked at each other for what seemed like hours, and I will never forget. I climbed down the tree to the front yard, grabbed my bag, and together we raced down the street, running through fields and searching for darkness. We clung to the darkness for days, living in the shadows, travelling at night. A few days later, we were in Portland."

"Did your dad ever try to find you?" Tamika asked.

"If he did try he failed, so I'm not sure. We stayed in Portland for a few weeks, bumming money on Burnside, thinking we would find a place to live there. We had no plans to go anywhere else...then Jobie spent a weekend in Eugene. Before we knew it, we were staying in Eugene. Jobie really liked it there, I didn't. Too many hippies. Too small. I like living in the city. After about a month, we found a ride down to Berkeley. At that point, we decided that we would simply travel from city to city, state to state. Leaving was the hardest. The rest has been easy."

"Do you always agree on your destination? Do you ever argue?"

"We try to give each other plenty of space," he told her. "I tend to be a loner, I like my personal space. I need privacy. I tend to not mix well with others. I obviously don't fit in on the Drag."

"Do I bother you?" she asked.

"Actually, not at all. Now, Treva bothers me."

"How can you not like Treva?" she asked. "She is always so happy, always laughing."

"But she never laughs at anything funny!" he pointed out. "She just laughs. I mean, how weird is that?"

"What do you think of Austin?" she asked him.

"I like it." He looked down the length of the coffee shop, at the dark and empty stage at the far end of the balcony. The ceiling was naked with crisscrossing patters of wooden planks like the ribcage of a gutted carcass. The blocky metal tubes of the ventilation system clung to the bottom of the wood blowing cold air upon them. "The Drag isn't my scene, but Jobie seems to like it. It works for now."

"I don't think I fit in well here, either." She glanced out the window once again, seeing the same cars still lined up in traffic. The Eckerd sign suddenly lit with an electrical glow. Its light reflected in the water droplets on the windowpane, sparkling like glitter. "Where are you going after New Orleans?"

He smiled. "Who knows? We'll decide that at the time."

"Sounds like a blast. I should do something like that someday. I could just leave here, and why not?" She let out a deep exhalation that determined defeat. Her enthusiasm had completely derailed, her slumped shoulders and poor posture revealed this. "I'm not sure I could do it on my own."

"Why don't you join us, then," he offered loosely as he tapped the metal tabletop with his silver claws.

Her eyes widened with excitement. She could hardly believe it. "Really?"

He nodded casually.

She stared down at the old wooden floor, deep in contemplation, high on flattery. She was astounded, practically coming out of her dark skin. She looked up at him and smiled with all her straight teeth perfectly visible. "Yes, I'll go. But what will we do?"

"What are we doing now?"

"Wow...I've never been anywhere before...I've never even left Texas before!"

He smiled politely. "Here's your big chance. So what were your plans?"

"Right now or down the road?"

"You tell me," he told her.

"Someday I want my own home," she revealed with a pleasant smile. "A nice home. It wouldn't have to be big or fancy, just a nice house. A house, not a trailer."

He stirred his drink patiently as a smirk formed on his porcelain-white face. "Go on..."

"I want...maybe a dog, one that won't run away."

"What color is the house?"

She was quick to respond: "White."

"A fence?" he asked.

"Haven't really thought of that..."

"Well, think of it—a fence?"

"I guess not," she decided quickly. "Lots of trees, though."

"Would you want kids and a husband?"

"Oh yes," she replied. "Without any doubt I would."

He watched her as she fell into a deep state of introspection. She seemed at ease, it was the first time he had seen her this way. "Since when have lesbians sought husbands?" he asked.

She smiled.

"Busted!" he proclaimed proudly.

"Men don't like women like me," she explained disparagingly.

"What exactly is a woman like you?"

She shrugged her shoulders. "Men like waifs, they don't like fat girls like me."

"Actually, men don't like a shitty self-defeatist attitude like that."

"Well," she exclaimed, "it's the truth!"

"The truth is that you can be what you want to be. Look at me, every day I redefine who I am. I am the artist and I am the art. My expression, I'm like a statue. When I stand in front of a mirror, I can be the person I want to be. If you think you're overweight, then lose it. People do it all the time, why should you be an exception? You're as great as you want to be, and as worthless as you allow yourself to be."

"It's not that easy," she told him.

"Is it easier to just bitch about it? You're a beautiful person, Tamika. Share what you have with the world. It's such a colorless place anyway. Look around you, look at the sullen faces that fill the world. What better reason to have confidence than to simply accept that *no one* has it. That's the best reason I've found! How does that old song go...*wear your love like heaven*. You have so much to offer, there is so much color inside you just waiting to explode like an orgasm of rainbows. Let it out, liberate yourself."

She smiled at him, absorbing his kind words toward her. "I have a gift for you," she announced. "Do you want it?"

He nodded excitedly as his deep purple lips twisted into a very genuine smile.

"It's nothing fancy," she told him as she dug into her pillowcase of items. She pulled out her plastic baby doll with fair skin and no hair. "Here, it's yours...my best friend gave it to me, and I want you to have it now."

He slowly reached up and took hold of its waist, tenderly pulling it from her hands across the glass, cradling it in the clutches of his silver claws. "It's great."

She smiled happily.

"These clothes have got to go," he resolved with an impish sigh as the doll relaxed itself on the spread of his black gloves. "Can I dress it up?"

"It's yours," she said. "You can do whatever you want with it."

"I'll make it my own offspring, then," he said as he smiled from across the table. His warmth radiated through the layers of ivory make-up that covered his face. "Thank you."

1:46pm

Droplets of water covered the bumper's chrome like an assortment of lost contact lenses. Jobie ran his thin finger along the cold surface, peeling away the water like sweat. It streamed down his arm, zigzagging like a snake before descending from his elbow to mud-soaked asphalt.

He slid forward from the curb, dropping himself on the edge of the street. The backside of his kilt absorbed the stagnant mixture of oil and rainwater from a small reservoir of stench trapped between the cracks of the dilapidated asphalt. A blue plastic bottle cap floated in the murky little pool, seemingly drawn to him like a life-raft seeking refuge from the filth and decay. He picked it up and examined it, noticing an inscription on the hidden underside. It read *You Are Not A Winner.*

Across the street, small children ran wildly in circles on the small lawn of the University Baptist church daycare. Black metal bars restrained the children from the world, or was it that the bars restrained the world from the children? Jobie assumed the latter by how the elders nervously watched him. He imagined what they saw in him. He liked what he assumed they feared, finding comfort in the murkiness of their prejudice. There was safety there, a guaranteed distance from vulnerability. The irony was that he would give anything to be behind those bars. He had been taken away from such comfort at too young an age. As he watched them frolic with bliss and disregard, a wave of remorse swept over him. The safety of those confines, he could scarcely remember his own comfortable structure. The cage through which he now peered, it wasn't constructed from love, but rather fear and hate. Those children, he thought, they would spend their entire lives trying to return to this. Now, for him, it was too late. He was a monster, what the parents feared most, yet the reality was he had never changed. Only they had.

"What are you doing?" an innocently sweet voice asked over his shoulder.

Before he could turn, Treva plopped herself gleefully on the curb.

"Why are you sitting in a puddle in the street?" she asked.

"Why not?"

"What are you doing?" Her soft, feminine voice blended with the children's innocent chatter.

He shook his head loosely. It was a stern, confident gesture. "Nothing."

"I've met some people," she announced quickly. "I like it here."

"Don't get attached, we're not staying." He turned to face her, peering into her eyes. She smiled at him. His tattooed face was straight and narrow.

"You never smile," she pouted. "Why do you never smile at me?"

He looked quickly over her shoulder to nothing, anything to lose eye contact. "Why do you ask questions like that?"

She shrugged her shoulders. "You never smile..."

He turned to face the children once again. Knowing she wasn't watching, he smiled, but only to himself.

"We're going out tonight!" she exclaimed loudly with a deafeningly sappy voice. Sweetness seemed to pour from her mouth like sugar.

"Where?"

"Um...I forgot, but I have a flier right here," she told him as she searched each pocket. "Right here...Ohms...they're actors or something...they're called Skin Ensemble. Not that I care about that, but we're scoring some acid. We're supposed to meet someone named Talon, we'll need to tell him that Dickhead sent us."

"Who is Dickhead?"

"That's who I met...that's what I'm trying to tell you," she said irritably as she extended her arms in the air. "See, you never listen to me..."

He shook his head as he sighed loudly. "Who is Dickhead?"

"Some guy."

"Some guy?" he asked as he turned to her quickly with a sharp eye.

"Yeah...just some guy. Why?"

"Why are you trying to meet other guys?"

"Why not?" she asked.

"What am I here for?" he demanded. "Why are you even hanging out with me, then?"

She sat quietly.

"Why?" he repeated.

"Don't talk to me that way, Jobie," she mumbled uneasily. "I don't know...everyone knows him down here. On this corner, he seems to be the one who watches after things."

Jobie laughed coldly. "Watches after things?"

"Seems that way. He kind of has a gang, they fight another gang called the Straight Edges."

Jobie laughed. "Straight Edge is not a gang...this guy isn't in any gang...he's just trying to get into your pants."

"I don't know," she returned quickly as she raised both hands out to the humid air once again.

"Sounds like he earns his name, if you ask me," Jobie decided.

She shrugged her bony shoulders as her thoughts wandered a different path. "What was the name of your hometown again? I forgot."

"I've told you."

"I have a lot on my mind...I'll remember this time."

"Tacoma," he said quickly as he stood, disappointed. "Puyallup, Washington." He reached in his sporran and pulled out six rocks. "One from each state I've been through."

She reached out her bony hand. "Let me see them."

41

He grabbed her hand with his other, holding it for a second to see her reaction. She clamped hers around his and smiled at him.

"Can I see them now?" she asked politely, patiently.

He nodded as he placed them in her hand. He watched as she studied each one, drinking his past, wishing she had been part of it then. He loved watching her, memorizing her warm smile, consuming her cheerful disposition.

"Can you tell where each is from?" she asked as she raised one to him. "This one?"

"Arizona..." he said quickly. "I got it about three minutes after I met you. It was right out front of the record store. It's my favorite one, it reminds me of you."

She smiled. "And this one?"

"Oregon. Before I met you."

She laughed. "So are these marked by whether or not you knew me yet?"

"Basically," he admitted.

"Is this everything you own?"

"No," he told her swiftly. "I have my writing and a book I stole in Tucson by Howard Zinn."

"Really? You stole it?"

He nodded proudly. "All property is theft anyway." He watched her as she contemplated his words. It made him feel proud, as if she were acknowledging something about him, maybe his intelligence, but he wasn't really sure. He just knew he liked it—her thoughts, his words. "I keep it hidden along with my writing, I don't want anything to happen to them, they're all I have."

"I see," she said. "Man, I could sure use a cigarette. Those kids are loud...they annoy me."

"Then I must annoy you," he told her. "Who is Dickhead, point him out to me."

She rolled her large eyes. "Why do you keep asking that?" She looked over her shoulder, down 22nd Street. "He's not here. If you want to meet him— "

"I don't," he said as he swiped the rocks out of her hand. He turned and walked away, leaving her alone on the curb. He glanced briefly at the children behind the bars and thought of what he'd give to go back, anything to go back.

Jobie slovenly leaned against the bar, cleaning the dirt from underneath his chipped black fingernails. Tiny red and blue Christmas lights were strung over the bar, painting the air a mixed violet. Black neon lights bathed the sparse white clothing of the other patrons in a purple glow. The venue was dark with misty smoke clinging to the stale air. Silhouettes danced somberly like ghostly apparitions on the nearby dance floor. Opaque was among them.

"Should I get my fortune told?" Treva playfully asked Jobie. She was perched on a barstool, pointing to a nearby table covered with stones. She read aloud the sign over the table: "Rune...Stone...Fortune...Teller." She repeated it twice to herself. She kept her wandering eye on the long line of people waiting to pay five dollars to receive a flogging from Mistress Lakasha. A shirtless man stood before her with his extended hands cuffed to the wall by chains. His head was bowed and his muscular back streaked with red welts from the tresses of the cat-style whip.

"They'll tell you that you'll be going to New Orleans soon," he told her over the gritty pulse of Industrial dance music. He glanced over at the fortune-teller. A wineglass sat at the center of the table. In it was a candle with most of its red wax melted into liquid like red wine. Red wine, with a flame dancing on the surface.

"Just you and me going to New Orleans?" she asked. "That's what I see. I feel like we'll be leaving Austin alone."

"You'd have to ask the bitch with the stupid-ass rocks." He looked out at the dance floor to find his brother. He could sense the attention that Opaque seemed to absorb from those who surrounded him. He was sporting a skin-tight leather outfit that accentuated his body's frail form with satisfying results. His arms were wrapped with tight fishnet that extended from his shoulders to his fingers. His face was flushed white with base and his red eyes seemed to be floating in a cesspool of black eyeliner. It was an unspoken rule of his to avoid color while out clubbing. Only black and white, latex or leather.

Dancing close to Opaque was Tamika, hovering over his every move. The DeeJay booth towered over the dance floor with an open wire mesh screen surrounding it like military netting. Two iron cages stood before the DeeJay booth. Pale young girls with bobbed raven hair danced inside them, wearing only black leather bikini bottoms and a single strip of electric tape across their nipples. Large speakers hung from links of chain with radioactive symbols painted on each. There was a girl with long, pink dreadlocks controlling the center of the dance floor. In each hand she gripped a length of chain, the ends of which burned in bright flames. She twirled them around her body and over her head in unison like bayonets. The orange glowing orbs of fire circled around her rhythmically like fireflies.

On the back wall of the stage was a large screen displaying a grainy black and white film's negative of a vivisection interspersed with transsexual pornography. It was difficult to distinguish the images from another based on the low quality of the footage. Blue orchids lined the front of the stage that contained only a single metal chair.

The music throbbed with an irritating screech, mechanical in origin with the accuracy of a computer. It was a systematic pulse, clamoring like machinery, droning. Heads bobbed and bodies slithered, grinding to the methodical rhythm as white stage-lights exploded with blinding intensity. Then suddenly darkness. The room was invisible, lit only by random candles as the rhythm of the machines grated into a convulsing surge of power like the passions of an android orgy.

On the screen behind the stage were the letters *The Skin Ensemble* glowing a faint gray, barely visible. A sullen silhouette of a man stepped onto the empty stage, followed by a woman. The crowd edged close to the stage, standing before the blue orchids. Smoke rolled onto the floor, rising in a swirling haze.

A flash of light ignited from the stage floor like a fiery fountain. In its glow was a tall and lean man wearing only a pair of leather jockey shorts and crisscrossing leather straps that were joined with silver hoops from his navel to his chest. His face was ghastly, near death and painfully thin. His eyes were closed with only the concave of his sockets painted with black eyeliner. There was no trace of hair on his head, including his eyebrows—completely waxed. A tattoo of a snake seemed to slither down the middle of his head like a mohawk. The tongue of the snake split in place of his widow's peak, lapping at his narrow forehead. Its green rapturous eyes were clearly present, even in the stark lighting. He slowly raised his hands outward from his body as the music grated around him. He appeared ominous and evil, like a servant of the underworld, fresh from death. In his hands were two leather floggers, and as he slowly raised them over his head, the tresses covered his face like a leather veil. The music stopped and the lights went out again. The crowd cheered with lewd anticipation.

Treva assumed this mysterious person was whom she had come to meet, Talon. Treva stared with unbridled enthusiasm, eagerly awaiting the return of light to her world. She wanted him to use those whips on someone, she wanted to see their pain. Her breathing became irregular. She squeezed her legs tightly together as she imagined being on all fours in front of him with an arched back, submitting to the leather. She yearned for the structure of the lash.

The music returned, grinding, throbbing...lapping at the audience with swift strokes of brutal punishment like cold metal on hot, sticky skin. The lights exploded once again, revealing two topless young girls bowing at Talon's side. With an unyielding expression and a calculated sense of motion, he advanced toward them.

He grabbed the bleached hair of the first one, coiling a hard fist in her clean hair. He yanked her head back forcefully, albeit gently. She looked at him uneasily, though perfectly relaxed. He moved his lips close to hers, slowly, passionately. He stopped within an inch, keeping her edged with desire as she stared at his mouth. He gave no expression, and no indication of a single thought. He then spit on her face and yanked her head so that she stared helplessly at the ceiling. His saliva dripped from her chin as he pulled his other hand back over his shoulder, lashing her back with his leather flogger. It cracked against her frail skin, ringing clearly over the music that scratched its way through the club's stone walls. She arched her back with desire as he pulled her head close to him once again. He leaned over her and stuck out his tongue, allowing his saliva to drip down into her open mouth. He relentlessly whipped her across the back several times, forcing her to grimace in painful desire. He let loose of her hair and stepped forward to the other young girl.

She stared at him uneasily, though she seemed strangely anxious and excited. A smile worked its way into her expression until he slapped her gingerly across the face. Her expression changed briefly, then the smile returned. She beckoned the scourge to be repeated. He gave it to her, leaving her cheek rosy red. She craved more. He could sense this, and therefore he returned to the other girl, leaving her wanting, frustrated with desire.

He swiftly grabbed the blond by her shoulders and raised her to the metal chair. Twirling his flogger in his hand, flexing his pale muscular body, he looked up at the audience that gave their undivided attention. With tremendous force, he slashed the tresses across her body, leaving a red streak across her flat chest. A second blow wrapped around her ribcage, staining her side with a throbbing bruise. His strike was otherwise precise.

As the music lost its momentum, so did he. He left her propped against the chair with her petite hand dangling passively to the floor. Her chest was lined with red streaks like a grid.

The lights faded quickly as coldwave music swiftly changed the mood. Tension filled the air with awkward enthusiasm. Slowly, red lights flooded the small stage. Talon was on his knees with his hands behind his back. His body was speckled with sweat. It dripped from his brow onto the stage. The young girls were gone. He was alone, kneeling in a pool of red light with his head bowed to the ground.

An Asian woman glided onto the stage, shifting her hips from side to side with a saucy sway. Her black hair was straight and long. A tight black latex dress was all she wore, though generously revealing it was. Over her small chest was a pattern of tattoos of leopard spots that crawled up around her neck and down the spine of her back. Just how far they went was only decided with a strong imagination.

She leaned down to his bald head and licked the sweat from his hot, clammy skin.

As the aggressive Industrial beats ignited once again, she raised her hand, holding up a silver hook to the crowd's delight. A white string dangled from the end of it. She brought the hook to her partner's skin, caressing his muscular back with its cold metal surface. Her black hair fell over her pale shoulders, arriving on Talon's hairless head. She suddenly sunk the hook into the pale skin of his back, releasing a small stream of blood as she shoved it through and back out his skin. His expression maintained like a statue as she yanked on the string, pulling his skin firmly. She raised another hook to the riveted crowd. Without hesitation, she plunged the hook into his skin on the opposite side of his back, allowing the blood to drip down his spine. She bowed to her knees, licking the blood from his body, cleaning the wounds with her tongue. She glanced up at the crowd with red lips that seemed to drip from her mouth, down her chin. Her face was free of feeling, free of emotion. It aroused the crowd. It aroused Treva. Her hands became coiled fists as she squeezed her legs tightly together, grinding them against each other under the bar.

"This is some fucked up shit," Jobie mumbled to her.

Treva nodded slowly as she moistened her lips with her firm tongue.

The Asian woman yanked upward on the hooks, forcing the man to his feet. She pulled his face to hers. They stared into each other's eyes longingly before she revealed to him a long silver needle. She placed it in his hands before kissing him. With their lips locked, she lowered the needle between their noses, firmly through their overlapped lips. The crowd cheered as they remained pierced together, connected by the needle. The music grated and the lights diminished around them.

The Skin Ensemble show was over.

The music continued with its blistering madness of modern mechanized grit. The dance floor filled once again.

Treva grabbed Jobie's hand, pulling him to the stage. She led him through the darkness with her hormones piqued by desire, finding the foot of the stage amongst the blue orchids.

Green lights suddenly lit the stage, sending a glowing hue through the club's artificial fog. Treva looked up only to find Talon towering over her, looking down upon her with hollow eyes. Two holes dripped fresh blood from his lips onto the blue orchids.

"You have something we want," Treva screamed in vain over the music. "Dickhead sent us."

He crouched to the edge of the stage, showing recognition of her statement. He grabbed her hand and pulled her up to the stage, leaving Jobie alone with his Asian partner. Jobie climbed the stage as Treva was cavorted off to the rear by Talon. Jobie stood next to the Asian woman, staring at her. She could sense his confusion, though not a word came from her bloodied lips.

"I liked the show," he finally told her.

She stared at him evenly, not even blinking.

He looked to the ground, waiting uncomfortably for Treva to return. "My name is Jobie."

She simply stared at him, allowing the blood to drip from her chin onto her latex outfit. He followed its course, watching the blood trickle down her sweaty chest.

"Nice tattoos." He wasn't sure if he was speaking to a human or a machine. He decided on a different approach to instigate a reaction from her otherwise tacit front. "I like your tits, can I see them?"

She shook her head evenly.

"Do you have a name?" he asked.

She stared silently, unmoved.

"I said I like your tits, can I see them?"

She shook her head again.

Treva emerged through the darkness with a silly-girl grin. She wandered across the stage, smiling shamelessly into the crowd. She shot a fist into the air as she stepped up to Jobie. "Score!" She held out four hits of acid. "Where is Opaque and Tamika?"

"I don't know," Jobie said. "Give them to me, I'll find them. These people are weird."

Treva placed the small cutout papers in his hand, taking one for herself and placing it on her tongue. Jobie wandered through the crowd, seeking out his brother and Tamika.

Talon grabbed Treva's bony fingers with a tender grip. She looked into his eyes, wading through the darkness of his soul.

"I liked your show," she giggled innocently to him.

His face was coarse and hard, frozen. The blood colored his lips like cherries. He softly gripped her fingers. His Asian counterpart stood at his side somberly.

"I understand it," Treva said, not fully knowing what her words meant herself. "The discipline over pain, it's spiritual, isn't it?" The cold hardness of his eyes answered her question without words. "I'm Treva," she sang happily, introducing herself to both of them.

Talon pulled her hand, bringing her off the stage to a back room—a green room painted black. The Asian woman closed the door behind them, locking them inside. One light bulb dangled from the ceiling, sending hard shadows over their faces. There was a pungent odor to the room. The stench of it was sickening.

"Spiritual..." the Asian woman said aloud as he glared at Treva's bright eyes. "How far would you look to find God?"

"I don't believe in God," she admitted. "God wouldn't have allowed certain things to happen to me. Even if he existed, I couldn't believe in him."

"You don't need to look any further than this room to find God," Treva was told.

Treva raised a brow of disbelief. There was a silence that surrounded them, though the music vibrated through the walls. The stench of the room was revolting. And the bright light blazed over a scratched mirror, burning their tender eyes into tight slits. Treva felt like a tourist in their presence, though she wasn't sure where the trip would be taking her. The atmosphere felt synthetic, a byproduct of their ritualistic behavior.

"I don't even know both your names," Treva said with a throaty laugh. Her voice was trill.

"I'm Talon. This is Phaedra Lin." The timbre of his voice was like a raspy whisper. Barely audible, even in the awkward silence.

Treva bowed her head politely to Phaedra. The gesture was not returned.

Talon wandered over to a wooden desk. He opened a drawer and removed a small leather pouch. He returned to the two of them, standing uncomfortably close to Treva.

"You're right," he breathed softly to Treva. His soothing voice was hollow with what seemed to be indifference. "Spiritualism."

Treva smiled. "I suppose so. You're never really doing something bad until someone tells you that you are...right?"

There was no reply.

"I mean, that's why you do it," she decided. Her discomfort was numbing, she wanted nothing more than to leave, but something kept her. "Where is this...this thing that you talked about?"

"Thing?" Phaedra asked with a pointed glare.

Treva grimaced at her expression. She found her to be stunningly beautiful, it made her sick with jealousy.

Phaedra looked to Talon and nodded. He received her wordless thoughts clearly, and his own silent expression displayed his approval. He grabbed Phaedra's hand and pulled a hypodermic needle from the black pouch. He pricked her finger with it, digging deep into her skin until the blood flowed readily. Taking hold of Phaedra's wrist, he moved it to Treva's mouth, placing her bloody finger on Treva's limp lips. Treva stuck out her tongue, licking the fluid that soured her lips like salt. She sucked Phaedra's finger deeper into her mouth, drinking the blood, devouring it with a thirst she had never known. Talon lifted Treva's hand, piercing her finger with the needle, plunging it into his mouth, sucking the blood from the small wound. He punctured his own hand before placing it in Phaedra's receptive lips. Together they stood in silence, drinking each other's blood, feeling the life pour down their throats.

Treva's heart intensified its pulse as she licked and sucked on Phaedra's bony finger. The blood pooled at the base of her tongue, igniting her senses with sapphic prurience.

Phaedra reached up and grabbed Treva's upper arm, squeezing it tightly. She could feel the pressure of blood swelling in her arm. She closed her eyes and concentrated on Phaedra's digits that bled inside her lips. She felt a prick in her upper arm, shocking her. She opened her eyes to see that Talon had plunged the hypodermic needle deep into one of her throbbing veins. She gasped uneasily until the fluid entered her body. She could feel it moving up her arm, changing her entire chemistry into grand divinity. The gritty atmosphere of the poorly lit room suddenly transformed into the most beautiful place she could ever possibly imagine. She was surrounded by love—a hyper-orgasmic sense of love and being that was perfectly alien, perfectly perfect. Truly blissful, euphoric. The release of death couldn't be any better, heaven couldn't even be close...the vomit itself, warm and filled with blood, it was absolutely breathtaking...a trip to Eden, a dance with angels.

They were absolutely right, she had embraced divinity.

The following morning, she awoke on the Drag against a beer-stained wall that was tagged with graffiti. Her stomach ached and she felt she was truly in hell. Her comrades were at her side, fast asleep. Her body was quaking, and hives covered her body like acidic burns. She examined her arm briefly, realizing that Talon's pager number had been carved into her arm with a razor blade the night before.

She pulled herself to her feet uneasily. She was in hell, no doubt about it. She lunged herself forward at a pedestrian, grabbing an unsuspecting girl's coat and clinging.

"Please help me," Treva begged the horrified student. "I need to call someone, please...give me some change."

The girl reached nervously into her pocket and pulled out a modest handful of silver coins. Treva reached anxiously for it, knocking it all to the broken sidewalk. As the girl quickly rushed away, Treva fell to her knees and collected the change as her body ached and her mind struggled to control itself. She didn't want the control, she needed the loss of control. She owned heaven the night before...now this hell.

The anxiety of the craving caused her skin to splotch and discolor. Hives spread across her body like flames.

She desperately stumbled down the Drag to a pay phone where she dialed the pager number with maddening impatience. A lifetime passed before the call was returned. She picked it up on the first ring.

"Talon!" she screamed into it.

"Yes?" he breathed softly. His voice was icy and calm.

"Help me, I need help."

There was a brief silence followed with the sigh of words: "Where are you?"

"On the Drag, by Tower records."

"Do you have any money?"

"No," she replied defeatedly.

He paused momentarily. "Get money—you'll need it. I'll be down there in thirty minutes," he told her before he hung up.

"No, I need it now, I *can't* wait," she cried as she slid down the hard stone wall. "I need it now...*now*..."

WEDNESDAY, SEPTEMBER 16, 1998

The University of Texas at Austin
4:47pm

"I believe I'm done for the day," Chasey Novak told Vaughn.

He raised a stiff finger to request her patience as he finished the last paragraph of the article on the chemical components of Tea Tree Oil. He looked up at her and smiled while rubbing his bloodshot eyes. "It's been a long day."

"The day is not nearly long enough," she replied as she placed her clipboard on his desk amongst the copies of scientific journals. Her face was perfectly composed and relaxed, brimming with complete self-control. She was in her environment, amidst the chemicals, formulas, and grand visions of biological manipulations for the advancement of mankind. Her long straight blond hair was pulled back into a ponytail, wrapped with a baby blue scrunchy. A few strands had escaped and were dangling over her beautifully fair skin, clinging to her naturally full red lips. The color of her blond eyebrows almost blended with her skin tone, and her pale blue eyes seemed to be the entrance to a vast and impressive wealth of scholastic knowledge. Her white lab coat was immaculate, as were her khaki Docker's pants and Adidas jogging shoes. A gold crucifix hung around her neck, resting above her modest cleavage. "Do you have any idea when the samples from the Burdock root are going to arrive?"

"I'll need to contact Schtepp," he told her, a bit discouraged. "I was promised they'd arrive today."

"I can't finish my report until that package arrives."

He leaned back comfortably in his old wooden chair, feeling a sudden relief in his intern's irritation. He liked her diligence. It put him at ease knowing he could depend on her. She would make a fine biological researcher some day. "We're very close. The new serum with extractions from the Evening Primrose Oil and Capsaicin is, in my opinion, ready to be tested on human subjects. What we have at this point is practically marketable, regardless of the improvements we have yet to make."

"I don't believe it's ready, but that's just my humble opinion, and maybe I'm too cautious. The Burdock root," she interjected assuredly. "That will finish it. I just wish those samples..."

"I'll get on them. By tomorrow morning, no later."

"I'm sure you can't wait for this to be completed," she said to him with whimsical optimism. "This is your dream, after all."

He nodded proudly. "Indeed so. And no, I can't wait."

She laughed aloud suddenly, chasing her train of thought. "Your ties with Doctor Schtepp will be severed."

He smiled, sharing with her the thoughts they both agreed upon. "Poor old fool. What will he do without me?"

"Well, he does have that woman he speaks so highly—what's her name? Lucinda?"

"Ah, yes...Lucinda. I bet she's a looker," he joked.

"Ah, what's in a look? Beauty is fleeting. She's probably a very nice person."

"Probably so," he responded callously. "Well, have a good night. Any plans?"

"Church choir practice. In fact, I'm almost late."

"I just need to finish up here, I'll be another half hour at least. I need not keep you, you're free to leave."

"Okay, thank you," she offered politely before grinning sheepishly. Her coy expression was indicative of a rare comical thought, or as close as she came to it. "Will I see you at church?"

"Hmm...probably not."

She nodded her head, happy with her casually dull wit. "Well, I'll have you in my thoughts and prayers."

He didn't want to admit how often and under what circumstances he'd be thinking about her. "Take care."

The phone rang as she walked swiftly out the door.

"Hello?"

"Ah, you're still there," Schtepp breathed heavily through the phone. "I thought I'd catch you."

"Have you heard anything about the samples?" Vaughn snapped. "They promised me they went out overnight."

"Hmm..." Schtepp took a moment before replying as he savored the forceful determination of Vaughn's large voice. Every word spoken left him enamored by the simple eloquence and overall sophistication of his entire being. "I'll give them a call. Don't worry about it, I'll handle it."

"I would appreciate that," Vaughn told him flatly.

"Would you care to have dinner tonight?"

Vaughn sighed with irritation, though his words gave no indication of it. "Oh, not tonight, I'm afraid. Long day, I'd just like to watch a movie and call it a day rather early."

"I understand," Schtepp shrugged uncomfortably.

"How about your friend Lucinda? You could ask her."

"She's here right now, as a matter of fact."

"Well, then, I shouldn't keep you," Vaughn said. He thought a moment, wondering who she was, what she looked like, and why he had never met her before. He knew that there was some type of close intimacy involved because he could sometimes smell her perfume on him. Little did he realize that his visualization of the scene on the other end of the phone was far more intriguing than he could scarcely imagine.

"You're not keeping me at all," Schtepp replied softly with a pair of red painted lips. His skin was powdered and pretty, covered with a fair amount of blush and gaudy green eye shadow. A flowery blouse covered his large torso, highlighted with a pair of spongy foam breasts that were shaped like torpedoes. An orange skirt, starched and ironed, covered his stumpy legs that were fitted within a large pair of dark nylons. His free hand caressed the high-heels on his large feet— Lucinda's large feet. "Maybe sometime this weekend, then, possibly dinner at my place?"

Vaughn opened his desk drawer and reached in the far back, under countless scientific publications. He pulled out a wrapped three-pack of bondage magazines. "I've got plans all weekend, actually," he told Schtepp as he considered the assortment of S&M video rentals that awaited him at home. "Thanks for the offer, though."

"Well," Schtepp whispered gracefully into the phone as he reached down and picked up a package from Federal Express, "if the samples arrive after all, I'll let you know."

"Keep me informed," Vaughn said as he slowly, yet eagerly opened the plastic wrap of his sadistic magazines.

Schtepp smiled mischievously as he placed the package of Burdock root samples in his lap. Slowing the completion of the project only prolonged his time with Vaughn. He didn't need the money in the same way his colleague did, nor did he really desire the notoriety. The companionship was worth more to him than the professional foundation of their union and their supposed mutual goal. He knew it was his clout that Vaughn cherished—nothing more. He had his own ulterior motives. "I will deal with it, don't worry. You can trust me."

4:48pm

Wispy dark clouds rushed overhead, sliding under the belly of a gray evening sky. The clouds were too thin and sparse to hold rain, though they carried the scent of another miserably wet night on the streets.

Tamika sat quietly alone in the courtyard of the architecture building, sitting on the edge of a murky pool of filth that was once an impressive fountain. Pigeons fluttered in the palm trees around her, making horrendous noises as if warning of the impending storm that crept its way toward them. Gray feathers floated in the swarthy waters of the fountain, buoyant over the trash that lingered at the rust-tinged bottom.

The wind suddenly picked up, dropping the temperature several degrees. Tamika's velvet dress rippled in the wind, a wave of black flowing down her body. She watched the dress vibrate from the elements, feeling the cold wind raise the hairs on her neck. It felt like fingers running up her spine—thin, bony fingers that scratched for life, begging for recognition. Tamika whispered a soft *hello* to the open wind. Could it be Cindy's ghost, she wondered, still looking after her? Probably not.

The ripples glided across her dress like quivers from a post-mortem muscular reflex. The velvet was like a sea, and it surrounded her body until she became one with it. She was caught in its immobility, incapable of movement, unable to give the struggle for hope. There was nothing. Sadly, nothing had ever changed. This was her life, as it had always been.

She thought back to her lonesome childhood, of her negligent mother, and how often she was told that her life was an accident. Her existence was the worst thing that ever happened to her mother. She was glad to finally give the woman the peace she never deserved.

A long forgotten childhood memory resurfaced. It involved a bicycling accident one summer day. Though the injuries were minor—a scraped knee and wounded pride, the trauma of the experience held her in great captivity. She had been frantic, she remembered well the feeling of fear as she limped home, crying uncontrollably. As she reached the lawn, she stopped. Her sobbing came to a quick halt as guilt consumed her—her mother wouldn't want to deal with this. She looked across the street where the neighbor's truck was parked in front of the doublewide trailer. How her mother despised the Griffin family, with their well-kept yard and lawn ornaments and Sunday barbecues...she slowly limped across the gravel road, looking over her shoulder every few steps to make sure her mother didn't see her stepping onto enemy land.

Tamika rang the doorbell, feeling like a complete traitor as she stood sobbing with blood running down her leg into her cheap shoes.

"Ma," the eldest son said loudly as he stood over Tamika in the front door watching her cry. "Something happened to the fat neighbor girl..."

Tears ran down Tamika's face, but not from the pain, rather from the humiliation of cowardly running to strangers for help. She was taken into the bathroom, a luxurious place so unlike that which Tamika had always known as a bathroom. It was spotlessly clean, just how she had always imagined hers would someday be. All of the lights in the fixtures worked, and the toilet paper was actually on the roll with the paper going over the top, just as she thought it should. The room even smelled clean, somewhat like bleach, and somewhat like citrus fruit.

"What's your name?" the woman asked as she cleaned the wound with a cotton ball and hydrogen peroxide.

"Tamika."

"Is your mother not home right now?"

Tamika sat silently a while, but before she could answer, the woman asked, "Would you like some cookies? I just made a batch yesterday. Do you like cookies?"

Tamika nodded passively with a sniffle.

"What's your favorite kind?"

"The ones in the brown box," Tamika replied with a beleaguered whimper.

The woman smiled. "The ones I made are peanut butter. Do you like those?"

Tamika nodded again.

"I think you're going to live," she told her. "This was a doozy crash, but I think we can salvage this leg." She put a bandage on it, one with Ninja Turtles, it made her smile. "Okay, that's the smile I was looking for...now how about some cookies?"

The rain began to fall, landing on her black velvet dress, the cesspool of sorrow in which she could find herself sinking deeper and deeper.

"Tamika," a feminine voice whispered with the wind.

She glanced over her shoulder, scanning the dark. Treva's gaunt and pasty face smiled from the courtyard entrance, shining in the cold drizzle. She sauntered up to Tamika, standing over her, momentarily shielding her from the rain. "I need to borrow money."

Tamika immediately handed over two dollars in pandered change without hesitation.

"Once when I was still living in Colorado Springs, I was at this pond," Treva told her as she stared down into the murky fountain. The rain sizzled upon its water, pocking its surface. "There were some ducks down in the pond, and I was fairly young, I liked ducks, you know."

Tamika glanced up at her politely, attentively. She couldn't help but notice her dry and irritated skin. She seemed to be covered with tiny flaking scales. The rain, she hoped, would do her souring complexion some good.

"Suddenly the male ducks overpowered this female duck," Treva told her. "And they all took turns savagely raping this bird. But when the bird had the opportunity to escape, it just laid still, it didn't have any interest in getting away." Treva turned to Tamika and raised an eyebrow that revealed her tired, bloodshot eyes. "Have you ever craved pain?"

Tamika shrugged. "Not really."

"I believe humans instinctually crave pain. Consider the fact that in the course of human history, we've only been out of the caves for a fraction of that time. Of course, cavemen weren't able to buy a woman a drink at the local bar, they had more direct ways of getting action. For our species to exist, don't you think that there is something built into the design of women to crave this aggressive approach? If not, wouldn't all the women have congregated to the hills, hiding from men? I have this theory about women," Treva resolved. "Show me a woman who claims she isn't drawn to the idea of violently degrading sex, and I'll show you a liar."

Tamika sat quietly as the rain cleansed her body. She didn't want to lie.

"Thanks for the money," Treva said innocently before leaving.

9:10pm

Jobie stood in the shadows, drinking Lone Star beer from a bottle, watching Treva as she waited on the street corner. Every second that passed filled him with pain. He knew she was waiting to meet someone, and it wasn't him. He looked to the ground and kicked some rocks against the stone wall of the alley. In black letters spray-painted across the wall were the words *Chumps Rule*. The rocks ricocheted off the wall, falling to his duct-taped shoes.

A black convertible Plymouth Fury pulled up to the curb. Treva stepped forward and climbed inside. It was Talon and Phaedra. He poured the beer down his burning throat as the car slowly crept down the street with its red taillights aflame.

Propped against the far wall in the darkness was his small fortress, a stack of wooden pylons that held the shrine of *The Apolitical Manifesto*. He stumbled over to it, drawn as if it was the luring finger of his lover. His writing was the only thing in his life that had ever been true, that had never let him down. He leaned his weight against the pylons in silence as he clutched the bottle of beer. He also loved beer. Beer and writing.

Memories fixed themselves upon him. Not the typical ones of locker room torment and brash insults from the class elite, but the more recent memories of his journey to freedom. Treva's effortless smile as the desert wind whipped her raspberry hair in a furious mess. The way the freight train rumbled beneath them as they ventured eastward into the darkness. Jobie faced the rear, watching where they had recently been, uninterested in their direction. Behind Treva, a storm brewed on the western horizon, and the rain could be seen falling from the dark clouds onto barren mountains. The sun was setting behind it, visible only as a fractured blur of hot pink through the distant storm. Its color was a perfect match for Treva's hair. Its natural beauty also on par. The moment was a perfect start to a perfect end.

He remembered at the time feeling hopeful and optimistic, free from the past.

"Hey!" a raspy voice came from behind him. "Who's there?"

Jobie looked over his shoulder—he was startled—it sounded like his father's voice. Two young men, roughly his own age, stood side by side with crossed arms, blocking the entrance to the alley. One stepped forward, clearly marking himself the owner of the voice. His black shirt was tight and old, torn strategically, revealing firm muscle. His black jeans were of the same quality, and his cheap sneakers, equally so. His orange hair was messy and his face filled with anger. Acne scars covered his jaw like a beard. His friend, an obese mama's boy with thick glasses, long clean hair, and an *Evil Dead* T-shirt, stood with his hands tucked loosely in the pockets of his blue jeans.

Jobie dropped *The Apolitical Manifesto* down on the pylons as he stood to greet his visitors.

"Who are you?" the smaller, more rugged guy asked aggressively. His voice was gritty.

Jobie scoffed with a condescending glower. He crossed his arms to show his casual indifference.

"I asked you a fucking question," the guy said as he stepped closer, edged with explosive anger. "When I ask you a question, you answer. Got me?"

Jobie laughed.

"Do you know who I am?" he asked Jobie.

"Nah...you got it wrong," Jobie responded with a drunken slur. "The question is, do *you* know *me*? Obviously...you do not..."

His face ruptured with heated angst. He reached inside his pocket to retrieve a shiny steel butterfly knife. "My name is Dickhead. I'll tell you the deal...you will show respect." He closed the distance to where they could see each other's bloodshot and mutually hostile eyes.

Dickhead's partner stepped up beside him, besetting Jobie in the corner against the wooden pylons. Instinctively, Jobie smashed his beer bottle downward against the stone wall—a trick he learned years ago, it was the best way to get a jagged edge on a broken bottle. Its loud crash echoed through the alley.

"Come on," Jobie threatened as he raised the bottle to Dickhead. "Let's go, mutha-fucka!"

Dickhead shook his head, unamused by Jobie's drunken swagger. "Drop the bottle, I'll drop the knife. We'll fight like men."

Jobie shook his head. "Negatory, pal. Come on, let's go."

"There's two of us."

"And there's only one of me," Jobie reminded him boldly.

Jobie scooted forward, slashing the air with his broken bottle, swiping it within an inch of Dickhead's face. He saw no counter-attack, but felt the knife barely graze his arm as the blood quickly slipped off his elbow. He looked down at the wound just as a swift kick from Dickhead's friend sent him against the wall. He felt his face mash into the brick as fists rained upon him with violent force. With each impact, he could feel the numbing pain of blood and bruises coloring his pasty body. He covered his head as he slid to the pavement, cradling his body like a baby as they stood over him, kicking and beating. As he lay in a huddled mass, all he could see was Treva holding him tenderly, pampering him, loving him. She was nowhere around. He gasped for air as silence fell upon him. He felt alone, he had no idea where they were, he couldn't see anymore. His eyes were swelling.

The blows had ceased.

He felt warmth trickle down his face, over his neck. Urine. It burned his bloodied cheek like saltwater. It bathed him, penetrating his open wounds—he flinched and floundered against the wall of the alley, but he couldn't muster the strength to crawl away. He stopped resisting as he struggled to breathe, all the while feeling the piss stream down onto his face. Cold laughter filled the air, and he listened to them, laughing so proudly at his pain. His eyes were swollen shut. He envisioned Treva's uncalloused smile radiating through him, but she was nowhere near.

Through the ringing in his ears, he could hear footsteps. He cracked open a swollen eye and saw them strutting away. He placed his hands on the ground that was now saturated with their urine and tried desperately to raise himself.

"Come here!" he screamed desperately. He didn't look up,

but he could hear that they had stopped walking. "*Motherfuckers...*"

"Are you talking to me?" Dickhead squealed.

Jobie pushed against the cold cement, hoisting himself inches away from the ground. "Get back here, you...fuckers...I'm not through..."

Dickhead looked to his friend, then back to Jobie's beaten body. He shrugged his shoulders. "You want more?"

Jobie lifted himself to his knees. From there he leaned back against the wall, facing them with one eye slightly cracked open as he gasped for air. He could see in their expression that they had worked him over pretty well. They seemed to have lost their anger. Jobie hadn't, though. "Next time...you won't know...what hit you...motherfuckers..."

Dickhead grabbed Jobie's head and pushed him back against the wall. The impact ignited the pain of every injury. One last kick to the chest put him back to the ground. He could smell the blood in his throat, he could taste the urine, and he could see Treva's lovely face, smiling, full of love...her eyes cloudy with simplistic beauty and absolute joy for him. He raised himself again, he wouldn't fall, not for these guys.

"Ah, what's this?" Dickhead said in Jobie's blindness. "Must be yours."

Jobie could hear the tearing of paper as pieces of *The Apolitical Manifesto* showered upon him. He reached into his sporran as he looked down at the shoes that encircled him. He cupped the largest rock, the jagged California rock. It was long and slender with sharpened edges. He tucked it under his kilt away from sight. He crawled to the pylons that were now surrounded with ripped paper.

Jobie jabbed the jagged edge of the rock deep into Dickhead's calf. Caught perfectly off guard, he twisted sideways off balance from the explosion of pain. He teetered to the wall, holding his leg.

Jobie found the strength from adrenaline to lift himself to his knees, just in time to shove the rock straight into the other's crotch. The impact sent him back a few steps, crashing into the pylons, doubled over and near useless.

Jobie stared in amazement through his one good eye. He could almost feel the pain flee from his body. He struggled to climb to his feet to defend his honor. Then came the slashing of the knife, missing his face by only so many inches. As the knife cut at the air, he realized that he had only served to anger them.

Dickhead connected his left fist with Jobie's jaw, sending a fountain of blood from Jobie's bitten lip. He fell to the ground, held down by all the pain that returned with a vengeance. He was motionless in defeat, beaten and humiliated. Dickhead tucked the knife back inside his pocket and spit upon Jobie's bloodied face.

"Come on," Dickhead gestured to his sidekick. "Let's leave."

Thursday, September 17, 1998

Hyde Park
9:47pm

Dark shadows slithered along the cedar walls of the cramped study, born from the light of a gallery of lilac candles. An impressive array of collegiate books with bent spines filled the limited space of the boxy room. The books seemed to flow from the shelves, dripping into towering stacks of concrete knowledge onto a nearby wooden table. A small forty-watt bulb hung from a fixture that dangled over Vaughn's head.

Blossom Dearie's juvenile sweet voice crooned through a haunting rendition of Rodgers & Hart's *To Keep My Love Alive* from a small stereo in the other room. The song, about a woman who routinely murdered her lovers before the passion faded, was one of Vaughn's favorites, though the sentiment had temporarily lost its luster to an unfavorable mood.

His eyes squinted irritably as he reread the report. He paused briefly to take a sip of camomile tea as he contemplated its supposed urgency. *Risks of Compositional Contamination* by Chasey Novak. Her caution insulted him. Such nerve for a mere understudy to challenge his experience... He wasn't about to postpone the tests—they had come too far, spent too much money already. Time was not on their side—not with the increased popularity of herbal cures and antidotes. Experiments such as these were being conducted all over the world—the slightest delay could set them at a permanent disadvantage. The additional month requested by Chasey was out of the question. They were ready for the testing now. Any alterations in the serum's formula could be made along the way.

He placed the report on the armrest of his recliner while he took a moment to finish the cup of tea. He dangled the empty ceramic mug in his relaxed fingers as he glanced about the room for his own research notes. They were nowhere to be seen.

He closed his eyes, tense with frustration. The notes were still at the university, and with the hour approaching ten...it could wait until morning.

His deceased father's face flashed through his mind—not the face he had remembered as a child, rather the decrepit ruin of a man whose life was slipping away. It was a ghastly shell of a memory, a sick conclusion to an otherwise enviable existence.

"Son," his father said gravely, "I spent years in the field, I gave my life to my work." He paused a moment as he breathed slowly, summoning the air to finish his thought. "My name will soon be forgotten. I leave the world nothing...I leave only you." He pulled Vaughn closer. "You will be successful...my name will be remembered...through you."

"I won't let you down," Vaughn promised. "I give you my word."

Vaughn sprang from his chair with a rediscovered vitality. He checked his pockets for his car keys and quickly made his way to the door.

9:48pm

"Money first," Treva insisted.

The young student eagerly extended a dollar bill. She swiped it away quickly, tucking it inside her deep pants pocket.

"It's dark in here," the other, more cautious student complained as he gazed uneasily down the alley. "Step into the light."

She stared at him, hating the thought of succumbing to this or any other request. But she needed the money, her pride would have to subside. She took one firm step forward as she glanced down at her shirt, making sure that the light would in fact be on her body. "Ready?" Without waiting for a reply, she raised her shirt to her shoulders, watching their eyes widen at the sight of real bare breasts. "Do you want to see more?"

They nodded.

She put her left hand down over the crotch of her pants. "Want to see what I have in here?" She revealed the metal teeth of her zipper. "Ten dollars."

"Five," the less cautious one told her confidently, asserting his presence in a vain effort to control the situation. "You give me head, I'll give you twenty."

"You don't want her to suck your dick, man," his friend said aloud with perfect disregard. "She's probably diseased. Look at her, look how fucked-up she is. Look at her skin, something is wrong with her. You don't want her to touch you."

Treva looked down at her arm, at the rash that covered her body like rust. "I'll show you my pussy for five."

The two exchanged a glance before shaking their heads. "No, thanks."

Treva stared in disbelief as they turned to walk away. She couldn't fathom their lack of interest. It was a foreign tongue—venomous and scathing, poisoned with disinterest. She felt her skin crawl as though parasites were feasting on her flesh. She ran her fingers down her arm, scratching her skin until it pulled up under her nails in bloody streaks. The texture was coarse and dry, like that of a serpent. She impulsively scraped at her skin, shoveling it from her arm with brittle claws. She couldn't stop herself. Her skin blazed like fire, she wanted it off her body.

She slid to the blacktop, shrouded in darkness, thirsting for the impurities that deliver divinity in a charred spoon. She desperately needed money. She would do whatever was required to embrace the angels once again.

10:21pm

"Spare some change?" the grubby street kids recited glibly.

Vaughn turned reticent to avoid a confrontation. It angered him to see the depths to which the country had fallen since his youth. It was those damned liberal politicians that set the machine into self-destruct mode, he surmised, starting with socialized medicine, back with the New Deal.

As he lumbered down the back streets toward the university, he humored the idea of a vigilante ridding the streets of these vile iconoclasts. There is no life without purpose, he figured, yet there is clearly no purpose in their eyes. Useless and lost, a debit to a once great nation.

His gait was quick and firm. Each step seemed absolutely deliberate with focus and meaning. He stared forward into the night, beyond the commonplace truancy of the Drag to his destination at the university.

He abided by a personal philosophy he termed *fundamental naturalism*, or the virtues of barbarism. He considered capitalism an extension of this, and thus the reason for its effectiveness. He scoffed at the notion that humans are inherently peaceful creatures. No other species on the planet kills for sport. Humans kill without purpose, humans kill for reasons outside of necessity. We do it because it's fun.

As he stepped foot onto the Drag, he pondered how easy it would be for someone to kill one of these malodorous runaways. He was surprised that it didn't happen more often. If he was in a particularly foul mood, he sometimes found himself sketching out the process of it in his mind—how he'd do it, and how he could get away with it. These kids had chosen this lifestyle. They had severed ties with their families to live out here. Their families probably didn't even know how to find them. Yes, it would be easy—and thrilling. Although with the distance he kept himself, there was no danger of temptation.

"I'll show you my tits for five dollars," a warm, friendly voice offered.

He stopped a moment, shocked by the flagrant words and youthful voice from which they came. He looked down to see a pasty young girl leaning passively against the wall. Her left arm was striped with the trails of bloody scratch marks. An underaged tramp. "No thanks."

"Then I'll give you head for twenty," she offered with her juvenile voice, sweet as candy.

His lips scrunched unevenly as if he had bitten a lemon. "Your frankness appalls me. Again, no."

She giggled. She liked the silver tint to his hair. Even in the dark, it was quite striking. His eyes had a subtle ferocity, and he had that look. That look that said *yes,* despite the firm resonance that gave weight to his words. "I'll do it for ten," she offered. "Just for you."

He glanced at her arm, at the red streaks that appeared as welts. Her skin looked like chipped red clay. Tiny specks of dried blood from recent needle injections dotted the bend of her arm. "Poison ivy?"

"Ten bucks," she repeated like a used car salesman. "Just for you."

He reached inside his pocket and pulled out his leather billfold. He thumbed through the bills, pulling out a crisp new ten-dollar bill. "I'll give you this money if you answer three questions honestly."

She nodded her head excitedly.

"You have to be honest," he demanded.

"Promise."

"Poison ivy?"

She shook her head. "Comes and goes with stress."

"It's psychosomatic?"

"It's nerves," she corrected him.

He smiled at her ignorance, though he didn't find it cute in the least. It simply gave credence to his presumptions of a deteriorating America. "Looks pretty bad this time."

She examined her own arm. She didn't like his questions or his condescending tone, but the bill that awaited her tenuous claws reinforced a more cooperative attitude. "It is pretty bad this time, but in one hour I will have the skin of a baby."

"Why?"

Her bright smile stretched across her dry face. "I'll be high again."

"Question number two," he said brusquely as he looked over his shoulder to make sure they were alone. He knew he'd need a greater lure than money. "Have you ever tried a pharmaceutical drug called dilaudid?"

"No. Chiva, nothing else."

"It's the cleanest high you'll ever have," he informed her.

She smiled, unsure of where he was going with all this. "Do you want to fuck me or what?"

"That's where the third question comes into play...are you busy this weekend? And no, I don't want to copulate with you...I value my own health." He pulled all the money from his billfold and flipped through the small stack of twenties. "I will give you thirty dollars to meet me tomorrow night, at which time I will promptly give you an additional fifty dollars. That's a total of eighty dollars. All you have to do is sit and watch the television while I take your blood and give you vaccines that will help cure your skin problem—cure it forever."

"What about the dilaudid?" she asked.

"We'll negotiate that later. I'll require your assistance often, if you're willing to give it. Maybe we can strike a better deal for future meetings."

"You're going to want to fuck me, aren't you? I mean...you want to give me a vaccine? That's it? I find that hard to believe."

"Why is that hard to believe?"

"That sounds like work. You'd rather work than fuck?"

He nodded with a straight face. "Different priorities. I live for more than a cheap thrill."

"Thrills aren't cheap. How can I be sure I can trust you?" she asked. "How do I know you aren't a serial killer?"

He shot her a devious grin. "I'll require a lot of blood work from you, but I sense you don't have problems with needles. You'll be dizzy and light-headed—that's the worst of it. Trust me."

She looked at his firm jaw and the gray beard that covered his sculpted face. His hands were powerful and strong. And the look in his eyes...he had that look. She had seen it before, and she knew it well. It wasn't pure or pious—there was a dark intent stirring in the shadows of his mind. It beckoned her with a raspy, wretched whisper of foreboding danger.

"There's a food stand on the corner of 24th and Speedway, right on campus," he told her. "Just a few blocks away from here. Do you know how to get there?"

She nodded affirmatively.

"Meet me tomorrow at six o'clock in the evening. I will return you to the same location at the same time on Sunday. Can you do this?" He held out thirty dollars. "Fifty more tomorrow night. Don't be late."

She snatched the money from his hands. "No more questions, mister."

"Nice doing business with you..."

She thought a moment, trying to come up with the appropriate nickname for which she would like to be identified. "Purty."

"Purty, eh?" he said with an involuntary laugh. "You can call me Professor Richter. This deal is exclusive to us, and only us— no one is to ever know. I'll see you tomorrow, Purty."

FRIDAY, SEPTEMBER 18, 1998

The Drag
3:11pm

The sensation of thorns scraping from underneath the skin teased and tricked Jobie's senses. It was a sensation he knew too well. He couldn't imagine another person more familiar with physical pain than himself.

He stirred his sludgy heap of navy bean soup—the bowl that Opaque was kind enough to have gotten for him from the Food Not Bombs van. Free food was always good food, he often said, but his boiling rage was struggling against his waning appetite. He felt he should be famished, he hadn't eaten since his confrontation with Dickhead. For that matter, he hadn't slept, either.

He set the bowl aside and looked up at the white painted brick wall over his head. A monster had been painted on it, a black rotund thing with a single eye splaying from a tendril that had over its comically beastly head the words: *Hi, How Are You?*

"Are you not going to eat?" Opaque asked without looking up at him. He was buried in a clean notebook, submerged in thought. Torn and maimed scraps of paper rested on his lap— the remnants of *The Apolitical Manifesto*. He had purchased a new notebook with panhandled money, an effort to bring life back to his brother's passion. "Eat the soup, asshole."

Jobie shut his eyes, concentrating on the needle pricks that caressed his feeble and beaten body. "I'm not hungry."

Opaque sat quietly a moment, trying to piece together the puzzle of mauled paper.

In his silence, Jobie suddenly fell onto the memory of a very fateful day from his past. He was in second grade, and comfortably part of a small circle of devoted friends. His parents were still together, although his father did drink quite a bit even back then, but it was a complete family that would pass any modern standards.

On this night that Jobie would never forget, his father didn't come home. There was a call late in the night, and his mother answered, but that's all he remembered. The next day in class, he learned that his father had been arrested. During a drunken conversation that turned sour at the favored watering hole, his father had come to blows with another regular patron. Jobie's father prevailed in the confrontation—the other man was hospitalized with a concussion and a couple of fractured bones.

Everything changed for Jobie from then on. His father's opponent also had a child, Tina Murrow, the heartthrob of the second grade. She was devastated, and held Jobie accountable for her sorrows. Petty arguments flared over the jungle gym at recess with all the students taking sides on a conflict that was far beyond their understanding. Jobie stood against his class, his reputation tainted by what would become Tina's year-long campaign to ruin his name. Her efforts were a success. He often wondered what his life would be like if his father's brawl had never happened.

Opaque looked across the street at the Dobie, a massive dormitory of aqua-blue glass with a mall and theater on the first two floors. A strange white mechanical contraption rested on top of the building like a dormant flying saucer. It seemed to tickle the underside of the ominous rain clouds. "Eat your food," Opaque mumbled again.

"I'm not hungry." He examined his arm where the blade of the knife had sliced him. A long, thin scab covered the wound with a dark purple crust. He was covered with the sort. He picked up the bowl again to show his appreciation. "Do you think that all the bruises and scars I've had in my life could cause permanent damage?"

"I doubt it," Opaque said as he tore his brother's thoughts from the crumpled paper that seemed to be covered with scribbles. He moved the pen across the new notebook with perfect legibility, transferring the words of the old rambling text with smooth precision. If anything, *The Apolitical Manifesto* would be a lot easier to read now. He glanced over at his brother, seeing the hateful scowl smoldering across his bruised face. "Tell me when you think this thing will happen," Opaque said, referring to the structural demise of the society caste system that his brother had written so much of in his journal.

"Within twenty years," Jobie said with a slight perkiness.

Opaque sighed with relief—he had taken the bait. He was so predictable, he thought, but he knew Jobie rarely had the chance to speak his ideas to someone who actually listened. "How will it happen?"

"Social revolt," Jobie said matter-of-factly. "The working class is slowly being edged out by computers. Within twenty years, computers will be the working-class. It will be like the Great Depression, millions out of work. There will be only an upper class and a lower class—things can't work that way."

Opaque turned to him, showing his interest.

"The only answer would be to dissolve the government that we now have and make a new one, a socialist government. At the age of eighteen, people who chose to continue their education would get a minimum allowance that would support their needs. As long as you educated yourself, you'd earn money, an incentive to better ourselves. That money in turn would be put back into the system through their purchases, which would then be filtered back out as a percentage—rather than taxed, the business owners would pay a percentage that would be redistributed back to the people in the educational program. So the money would be in a constant flow." He paused to take a couple bites of the bean soup.

"Who would own the businesses?"

"Individuals, just the same as it is now. The only thing that would change is that you'd have something to fall back on rather than welfare. It'd promote positive values. If you wanted to invest in a business, you'd go the same route as you would now."

"And the government would be like what?"

"The government would be a group of randomly selected individuals that would oversee the polls."

"The polls?" Opaque asked.

He shoveled a couple of spoonfuls of the soup into his mouth before replying. "Every issue would be voted upon by the people through the Internet. Therefore the system would truly be by the people and for the people. We'd all have a voice. Take the electoral college, for instance. Why on earth do we use such an archaic system in this age? We could vote on computers, then have the votes calibrated by one massive database for complete accuracy. It'd be easier for everyone, and way more effective and honest." He paused a while to finish the bowl of soup. "Besides, anyone who'd want the role of President is no one I'd trust."

"This is what I'm writing here, huh?" Opaque asked.

Jobie nodded with gleaming pride.

Opaque looked down at the empty soup bowl, then back at his brother. He watched as Jobie nodded his head in satisfaction, then the scowl returned forcefully.

"I'm going to find those guys," Jobie coughed spitefully. He eased himself back against the brick wall as his bruised and scabbed body screamed in vengeance. "They will pay."

3:12pm

Bleak deconstructivism. The interior designers of Urban Outfitters were obviously obsessed with the concept. The naked stone walls looked as though they had been swabbed with a mixture of turpentine and battery acid. Each corroded metal support beam was labeled with what appeared to be chalk, designating its function in some abstract numeric code. Japanese paper lanterns of varying pastels hung from the concrete ceiling. The pane glass front window was shattered evenly like a contorted web, intentionally broken for aesthetics.

"What do you think of this?" Treva chirped with a high and sweet voice as she held a pair of aqua-blue hip-huggers over her bony legs. Her plum hair was tied into two pigtails behind her petite ears. A thin black half-shirt clung to her body with a large silver star centered on her chest.

Tamika looked down at the tiny pants, making contemptuous gagging noises. "You'd look like a skeleton," she said with a subtle sarcastic bite.

"Since when have skeletons been blue?" She placed it back on the peg-board rack while her large eyes roamed the store. The metal steps leading to the second-floor caught her attention. The steps themselves seemed to have literally broken through the second floor, with the rusty wire frames fraying from the slabbed center of the concrete ceiling. Electrical wires and fixtures dangled from the depleted framework.

"How long did it take to make that?" she pondered aloud as she pointed to the ceiling emphatically.

Tamika started to follow the extension of Treva's finger, but was struck by the raw patches of skin that crawled up her friend's inner arm. "Do you have chigger bites?"

"Shhhh!" Treva said while ducking her head below the racks. "You can't say that in here."

"Say what?"

"You know...it's not right." She shook her head in disappointment. "You should say *chegros*. You of all people should know that."

Tamika's brow crinkled. "I don't think they're called *chegros*. I think chiggers is the proper word."

"Really?"

"Yeah."

"Hmm..." Treva focused on a display of zebra-striped handbags. "Are you sure?" She skipped forward three robust steps to a rack of half-shirts the color of ripe tangerines. "I could spend all day in here."

Tamika remained one step behind at all times, experiencing the thrill of shopping vicariously through Treva's immeasurable exuberance. She found it ironic that a store designed to cater to the counter-culture carried a product line almost exclusive to the waif look. Treva was right at home.

73

After rummaging through stacks of plaid skirts, Treva glanced upward into the glowing orb of the blue paper lantern dangling over her head. She found herself living in a fog between highs. She had lost her virginity to the needle, dined on the forbidden fruit, and sacrificed her soul for a brief glimpse into heaven. It was worth every second. If she could live the rest of her life high, she'd do it in a heartbeat.

"So how long have you been with Jobie?" Tamika asked her.

Treva shot her a bent face, not unlike one a child would make. "What?"

"Come on...it's obvious."

"What's obvious?" Treva asked. "Nothing is going on."

"I don't believe you."

"You don't have to," Treva resolved coldly. She picked up a black shirt with a pair of lusty red lips puckered on the front. "No, we've never even touched, and I've definitely never fucked him. Is that what you want to know, how he is in bed?"

Tamika cringed at the thought. "Not hardly."

Treva picked up another black shirt, this one with the number zero on it. "My lucky number."

"What's up for the weekend? Got any plans?"

Treva shook her head. The stubby pigtails flipped over her ears with each seismic head turn. "Not with Jobie!"

"With who?" Tamika pried. She scooted out of the way of other customers, bumping into a rack of dresses. She turned to the rack quickly, horrified at the thought of breaking something to bring all eyes upon her. It was there that she had finally found something in the store that caught her attention. A ruby red dress. It was made of thin cotton, knee-length with a conservative cut that would cover the shoulders. It was both elegant and casual. "Wow, look at this."

Treva leaned over to look at it, reaching out with her scabbed hand to feel the soft texture of the material. "Yeah, nice. Better save those handouts. It'd take weeks of bumming change to pay for this."

That didn't seem unreasonable to Tamika. It'd be worth it. "I'm sorry, what did you say your plans were? I was listening, honest."

"I didn't say yet," Treva reminded her with her baby voice. Her eyes tensed for a moment as she raised her arms between them. Her skin looked as tarnished as the walls, boiling red. "Look at me," she whispered helplessly. Her face wrinkled with stress as tears formed in her eyes. "Something is wrong with me, Tamika."

"What?"

"I don't know."

74

Tamika couldn't disagree, she did look ill. Her face seemed tired, her eyes mere watery slits, and her whole demeanor was beaten and bedraggled. "What are you going to do?"

Treva sniffled as she shamefully tucked her arms under her skin-tight shirt. The black fabric stretched tight across her bony ribcage like a washboard. "I'm meeting a doctor this weekend," she noted optimistically. Her voice boomed with hope. "He's going to fix me."

"Really?"

She nodded brightly, slapping her pigtails against her perky shoulders. "I hope so." Her expression immediately fell desperate and sour as if the curtain had suddenly dropped. Her world had suddenly fallen into an eclipse. Her entire body responded with fatigued tension. She craved the needle, she had to find a phone—the doctor, she would be meeting him in a matter of hours, and he had promised this other new drug. Could she wait hours for another fix, though? "God, I hope he can fix me."

"You're meeting him tomorrow?"

"Tonight," Treva whimpered. "I stay all weekend. Don't tell anyone—don't tell the two brothers, especially Jobie." Tears rolled down her prominent cheekbones, dripping to the concrete floor. The redness of her skin was suddenly alive like fire, blazing across her body. She would match the ruby dress, she could become one with it.

"I won't tell them, I promise." She could see the pain and fear in Treva's bloodshot eyes. She placed her large hand on Treva's gaunt, bony shoulder. "It'll work. You'll be as good as new in no time."

"I hope so," she sobbed. "God, I hope so."

6:13pm

Chasey pushed through the front door of the Bagel Shop, ignoring the *Closed* sign hanging on the door. She stepped forward to a gentleman sweeping the floors. The eerie noise of indiscernible music was playing loudly from the tiny speakers perched high up the walls over enormous pane glass windows. Its gritty pulse tensed her body like steel.

"You've closed already?" she asked nervously over the racket.

Frank turned, somewhat alarmed to realize he was not alone. "Oh...well, we can extend the closing time by a couple minutes...I suppose." He stepped behind the counter and turned the stereo off, leaving a cold silence that brought the two intimately closer. "What can I get you—there isn't much left."

She looked down at the racks, bare and mostly empty. "I was told you have good pumpernickel."

"Bottom rack," he instructed. He waited for her to bend down to check out the remaining items. As she did, her loose shirt gave way to gravity, allowing a clear view down the neck of clothing to her silky white bra. It was a common recommendation from male bakers to beautiful female customers—bend over to look at the prized items on the bottom rack.

"I work for a doctor at the university...he swears by your bagels. He says he comes in every day, you may know him. His name is Ronald Schtepp."

"Oh, of course!" Frank said. "So you're doing the whole skin thing?"

She quickly looked up at him, almost alarmed. "You know?"

"Oh, not really. No details, but he keeps me informed of the progress."

"Hmm...interesting. I don't know about the pumpernickel. How about a garlic bagel, please?"

"Of course," he said.

She rummaged through her loose change, sliding forty cents across the cold metal counter.

He looked into her eyes—quite an attractive shade of blue—and nodded. "May I ask a question that's probably none of my business?"

"What's that?" she asked, anticipating the request for her phone number.

"What exactly are you working on over there?"

She smiled. "I can't just tell you."

"Of course you can! What, do you think I'll steal your ideas? I make bagels, give me a break! You can be as vague as you want."

She laughed. "Well, it depends on which of us you're talking about."

"How about you?" he asked. "What do you do?"

"I'm a glorified horticulturalist," she told him as she looked over his rugged face. She moistened her full lips and gave him a warm smile as she flipped her blond ponytail over her shoulder. "I grow plants."

He nodded slowly, confidently. His eyes stared deeply into hers, practically through her. He made her feel vulnerable, though completely at ease. Everything about his face was strong, and yet so reasonable and seemingly understanding.

Very withdrawn, but she liked that in a man—it presented a challenge. He had the eyes of fire, she thought, but at the same time, she wasn't sure what that meant. Whatever it meant, he had them.

"I work with DNA." She chose to mask her interest with a steady forthright dissertation of fact. "We're taking known herbal cures for skin irritations and manipulating the DNA to bring out the components that relieve or cure the condition."

He lowered his brow in contemplation, perfectly unaware of the effect he had on her. "How do you know what is actually doing the work, chemically speaking?"

"That's the whole trick," she confessed with a smile she just couldn't contain, "we sometimes don't. So it's been hit and miss, mostly miss. Lots of guesswork. That's what my two colleagues do. They make the educated guess, I do what I can to bring results."

"So you're an intern?"

She nodded. "Until I can get a real job, yes."

"So if they make a lot of money by marketing this product?"

"Then I get credibility, nothing more."

"Really?" Frank asked, a little disappointed. "Doesn't seem fair."

"It's the way it works. Credibility in such a competitive field is nothing to frown upon, of course."

"So once you've messed with this DNA, you..."

"...I insert it into the gene and hope that the plant that is produced takes on the new characteristics."

Frank nodded hesitantly with a disapproving scowl.

"Yes, I'm not sure what I think of it, either...tampering with God's work."

"So how does it look?" he asked.

"How does what look?"

"God's work."

She smiled comfortably. "Magnificent. There is no question, this is all a very intricate design. There was a designer, I am certain of that."

"Did you ever question it?" he asked, looking at the silver crucifix hanging from a chain around her neck.

"No. Never."

"Are you getting close to what you're looking for?" he asked.

"Have I found God?"

He smiled. "No, have you found the right combination of chemicals?"

"Depends on who you ask," she said, eyeing her watch.

"I'm asking you."

"Me? Then I would say no. Not yet. Close, but not yet. I'm more patient than my colleagues, but then again, I have nothing at stake here. Before this serum is used on a test subject, there are some things that need to be considered. How to combine the different compositions, at what levels—all of them artificially manufactured, none of them naturally occurring in nature...I just don't know if we're there yet. We're basically constructing a new form of life, and that's not to be taken lightly. Then we genetically combine this new organism with other strands of alterations...in the end, it will be a concoction of various genes spliced and manipulated—a completely new strand of life with characteristics that we know nothing about." She thought to herself a moment before getting slightly uncomfortable. "I'm saying too much, aren't I?"

"Not at all, but I get the picture if you'd like to quit while you're ahead," he said politely. "It's safe between us."

She nodded as she stared into his eyes, deep and understanding. She waited a second before saying another word, wondering if he had any more questions, such as her plans for the weekend. There was only silence. "Okay, well, it was nice meeting you, I'm sure I'll come in again."

"I will look forward to it," he told her. "Have a good night...and your name was?"

"Oh, I'm sorry!" she squeaked in tone that was much higher than her voice had been. She cleared her throat and replied with a lower, softer whisper. "Chasey Novak."

"Frank," he said as he reached out for her hand. "Frank Smith."

She lifted her hand gracefully, letting her fingers fall inside his firm grip. Making contact with his skin excited her with a cold and refreshing chill. His smile gave some indication that there was a mutual feeling involved. She let go reluctantly and mouthed the word *bye*.

As she walked away, he stared at the smooth skin of her legs, creamy and pale. She was not his type at all, far too pure, far too pale, and far too blond. Yet he couldn't take his eyes off her. She crept into his thoughts for the rest of the night.

6:14pm

Treva stared out the windows of Vaughn's car, watching the scenery of Hyde Park pass in a slow blur. The houses and neighborhoods north of campus were quite unlike those of west campus. These were much quieter, yet at the same time less somber. Each lawn seemed to boil over with a colorful array of flowers and vines. She considered how much she'd enjoy sitting on one of these old porches some hot summer evening with a glass of iced tea and a fat spliff burning in her hand.

She was disappointed to see that Vaughn's old house was one of the few without a porch. There was actually very little to it, just a small boxy thing with the overgrowth of ivy that scaled the white walls. The twisted and gnarled oak limbs that spread like a canvas over the lawn kept it in a dark encompassing shade. The grass thrived underneath, shielded from the blistering heat of the Texas sun.

She followed Vaughn to the front door with only the chirping of birds filling the air between them. No words were spoken until she entered.

"Take off your shoes," he insisted with a deep and firm voice.

She obliged without question. "Can I get a tour of the house?"

"No," he returned fervently. He led her to a back bedroom as he slowly removed his forest green necktie, allowing it to dangle around his thick neck.

She sat down at the foot of the King-sized bed, running her fingers across the smooth fabric of the beige comforter. She looked about the room, admiring its calm atmosphere. It had a rustic feeling to it, with its wood walls and floors and oil paintings of windmills. Aside from the pine dresser, a wooden chair, and an old footstool at the end of the bed, the room was comfortably vacant. It was as if she was inside a large wooden toy box, which seemed only fitting under the circumstances.

Vaughn stepped up to the foot of the bed, towering over her. She gazed into his hypnotic eyes as she stretched out across the bed and ran her eyes down the length of his body. His clothes were stylishly impeccable—pinstriped slacks and a pale green button-up shirt folded to the elbows. His leather shoes were polished to the extent that she could see the reflection of the wood floors.

"What are we doing first?" she asked him. "Are you going to take care of my skin, or are you going to fuck me?"

He laughed coldly as he looked down upon her. "I believe you have the wrong idea."

"Do I?" she asked, discouraged with his taut composure. "Are you not taking care of my skin after all?" She unfastened her street-sweeper corduroy pants, letting the fly spread to reveal her cotton white panties. She pulled her thin legs out of the pants, one by one. Her legs were splotchy red, like she had been splattered with tomato sauce that had dried on her otherwise fair skin. She tossed her pants aside to the floor. She looked him in the eye as she spread her legs far apart on the bed, showing him the crotch of her panties. "Fuck me."

His laughter reduced to a calm smile as he watched her, making no movements of any kind.

Her eyes tensed into hard slits. "I want you to fuck me. *Now.*"

"I don't have you here for that," he told her with thinning patience. His resistance to her lustful behavior failed to wane. "I'm old enough to be your father, young lady."

She reached down to her panties, pulling the fabric aside to reveal her moist vaginal lips. She spread her reddish-brown pubic hair apart to give him a better view. Her succulent lips parted somewhat, revealing the interior of her pink flesh. It glistened in the soft light. She slipped one of her long fingers inside her vagina, digging deep as she exhaled uneasily.

Vaughn's face restricted—the stench of her was enough to turn a virile man celibate. "I am not going to be having sex with you," he repeated calmly. "I can *promise* that much."

"Are you gay?" She looked to the crotch of his stylish pants. "You aren't even hard."

His condescending smile quickly washed away.

Suddenly it made perfect sense, the entire scenario. He was impotent. His promise was sincere, he couldn't have it any other way. She smiled at him, rubbing herself as she devised a new conquest. "Either you fuck me, or I'm leaving—which is it?"

"You need the money, you aren't going anywhere."

"You think so?" she asked as she prepared to stand up. "I'll leave right now."

"Sit down," he insisted with his commanding voice.

"Make me." She stood to retrieve her pants.

"You can leave if you wish. In fact, maybe you should."

"Coward..." She was ready to call his bluff. She held up her massive pants that appeared to be the size of a small tent. "Will you drive me to the Drag, I'll give back the money. I doubt this vaccine would've worked anyway. Nothing else has."

"Sit down." He grabbed her shoulders tightly, aggressively as a sense of wild exhilaration ignited within him. He stared at her blistered throat. He fought the temptation to wrap his hands around her veiny neck.

She looked up at him and smiled. She had successfully chiseled away a portion of his stoic exterior. "You like this, don't you?"

He let loose of her shoulders immediately.

"You want to throw me down on the bed, don't you?" she asked with a smile. "You want to cover my mouth while you pin me to the bed, fucking me like a dirty whore..."

This was already more than he had bargained. "Please keep your filthy body off the bed again until you have taken a shower. I can show you the bathroom..."

She tossed her pants aside again and jumped back on the bed. Her nipples were hard underneath her white tank-top, and her pubic hair jutted out from the edges of the cotton panties. She wanted to provoke him, to yank him from his throne of self-control. She crouched on his bed, pulled her panties aside, and smiled mischievously as a stream of urine splattered down her legs, onto his clean beige comforter.

Appalled and stunned, he lunged forward with anger, grabbing her bony shoulders once again. He yanked her violently to the wooden floor with a dull thud of young bones. "You disgusting bitch..." He grabbed her face, staring into her eyes with wild, roiling anger. The veins in his neck thickened. "What is wrong with you?"

She smiled as she lay on the wooden floor, helplessly in his clutches. She reached up and grabbed his crotch. He was excited by all this, just as she figured. She assumed he was desensitized by *normal* sex, probably a porn addict. "What's wrong with *me*? You're getting off to this."

He released his grip, allowing her to fall to the wood floor again. "You've ruined my bed."

She huddled herself on the hardwood, staring up at the maelstrom of havoc sweeping his body. She was pleased to see she had finally tipped his reserve. "You're going to have to contain me better. Maybe you should tie me up, restrict me. Maybe you should bind me, gag me, humiliate me...then fuck me. Tell me you want it, you want to fuck me, don't you?"

He shook his head with disgust. His ears were bright red. When he looked upon her, he saw vermin. "You have a serious problem."

She could see the conflict of violent interests eating away at him like cancer. She wondered how far she could push him— would he even strike her? She looked over to the wooden chair in the corner and pointed at it with her bony finger. "Tie me. You can stick me in the bathroom if you'd like," the tone of her voice suddenly shifted from seductress to helpless victim. "I'll cooperate, I promise. I'll take your medicine, I'll be good...I just want the dilaudid," she revealed with desperation. "Did you get it?"

He nodded. He was stunned by the sudden and extreme change in her demeanor. His own composure shifted with the confusion.

"I promise I'll cooperate." She stood submissively and wiggled helplessly over to the wooden chair. She dragged it and herself into the bathroom.

He followed her, watching her sit passively in it next to the sink.

"Tie my arms," she requested. "Keep me high and I'll do what you say, I promise."

He glared at her with utter contempt. Her mere existence revolted him. He had no qualms with what he intended to do to her.

"I'll do what you say," she repeated limply.

He quickly left the room, returning with several green handkerchiefs. He proceeded to chasten her as requested, something he now fully agreed was the best approach. He tied her hands together with one of the handkerchiefs, then tied each hand to the back of the chair. He left the room for a moment, leaving her in silence fettered like an animal.

She could hear him shuffling things inside the refrigerator. He returned with a collection of vials in one hand, and a package of hypodermic needles in the other. Each vial contained a liquid of different color and consistency. Among those chemicals was the dilaudid, as he promised.

Her heart raced with excitement.

11:01pm

The black tires seemed to rip the water that glazed 4th Street. The white BMW crept forward, edging through the Warehouse District, the center of Austin's gay nightlife. Lucinda shot a quick glance into her reflection in the rearview mirror, smiling at the hot bitch behind the wheel of the sporty ride. Tawdry clip-on earrings hung from fat earlobes, sparkling in the dim light of the city. Her face was delicately painted to a fraudulent excess of formal frumpiness. She owned the look of high maintenance femininity—an image reserved almost exclusively for adolescent girls and Drag Queens seeking to embrace the pure essence of womanhood.

Highbrow intellectuals cluttered the walkway in front of Ruta Maya coffee shop as the smooth jazz poured from the deep chasm of a nightclub known as Cedar Street. Well dressed pedestrians—most of them in their late twenties, drifted back and forth across 4th Street, making an unruly mess of traffic.

Young gay men passed in front of the car, gazing inside, staring momentarily into Lucinda's lonely existence. Her eyes followed their paths across the street to a line that formed outside of Oilcan Harry's. Each of the men were doused in rich cologne, she could almost smell them from the street, all luscious and tasty and meaty. Their clothing stiff and new, their hair firm and prickly with gel. Fine specimens, they were. As the old saying goes, the best looking men in the world are bound to the hearts of other men. Lucinda would have to agree.

As the white sporty beamer scooted across the intersection toward Congress, she smiled with excitement. She felt so alive, so young, so careless, and so perfectly free. Above all, she felt pretty. Her dress fit perfectly, her feet were at ease in the platform heels, it was as though her costume for the week had been shed, tossed aside for her to flower over the weekend.

She gave another quick glance into her mirror as she winked at her reflection with a confident and robust smile. She glanced down at her passenger seat, at its emptiness. She would have to change that, she thought, as she turned north onto Congress.

11:17pm

Solid vines of steel ripped from the moist green earth in a single-file stretch like a row of crops. The peak of each black iron stem collapsed evenly upon each of the others in one unified link. They looked like lashes dripping with mascara. Yes, eyelashes, that's exactly what they were, Opaque decided. He logically knew it was merely the iron fence of the church, but on acid...they were eyelashes. And the street upon which he stood, the Drag, was the eyelid of the giant, the eye of the world. He was cautious to not make a single movement that might stir and awaken it. How enormous the eye must be, and penetrating—he feared what the eye would know. He glanced back up at the fence, watching the blurred tracers of dark nocturnal images blend in his shifting field of vision. The lashes, yes. Deep and black, but not the black of colorlessness, rather the blackened void of non-existence. To touch them would be to become a part of them, to become nothing. He had been nothing once. He had no memory of the world before his birth, and thus, he did not exist, not before the seventies—so why believe that he did now? How could he be certain that he was no more than a shadow, or a stain, or even a character in some book, brought to life only on a black and white page, existing only in the mind of the reader? He couldn't be certain...

A car passed down the street, consuming his attention with its blinding lights and roaring engine. It seemed so alive, so much more so than he was. After all, he was simply a machine, a product of the earth with the curse of self-awareness. Why had he never thought about the air that he breathed, exactly what he takes inside his lungs every second...and those sounds, they must always be there. Why does he never hear them? The buzz in his ear, the sound of leaves slapping one another with the wind, and those dogs barking. Everywhere, dogs barking. What were they saying to each other? Warnings of impending doom? Do dogs bark in the same language?

He stepped back onto the curb, onto the eyelid of the giant, onto its gray, solid skin. What a mess we've made of the earth...dogs barking everywhere. He looked upward, surprised to see a row of stars peeking through the gray clouds that seemed to spread like a tear in cloth, as if the whole sheet was tearing, and that buzz in his ear, it was from the stars. That's where it came from, he could hear them, the gaseous explosions of distant suns, carried with the solar winds...another car turned the corner, easing slowly through the darkness, its white surface shiny and covered with thousands of water droplets. It gave it a bumpy texture. He thought that the car had acne—yes, it was covered with zits. No, lesions. Cancerous lesions. Soon it would be dead.

The window rolled down, and an older woman stared at him with a smile. Her face was hard and haggard, rough and aged.

"Hello," came the somber voice with a deep and quavering fullness.

This was a man, Opaque realized suddenly. Typically, he'd have noticed immediately. He nodded his head slowly with wide eyes. It was an expression that was intended as a polite greeting.

"My name is Lucinda," she said. "Want to go for a ride?"

Opaque stared at her, watching her with his blazing red eyes. "Where?"

"You tell me," Lucinda offered boldly.

Opaque threw his hands in the air, uncertain about where he'd want to go—of all the places to go, where would he want to go? He thought a moment. Maybe he could go to the store to get Pixie Sticks, different flavors to bring color to the sidewalks— who was this person? Did he know this person? What was the question? Did he know this person? He looked down at the black tires, wondering what would happen if the eye of the giant—the car looked ill, it would not live long. "Can we go to the store?"

Lucinda smiled, wetting her thick lips. "Anywhere you want."

Yeah, the store, he needed a marker for the doll, it needed lipstick, the doll looked too—who was this person? "Do I know you?"

"Not yet."

Opaque stepped forward, looking inside the car. Its interior was black and dark, and the seats seemed so deep. Would he be able to feel the ground passing below him at such a depth? Of course he would. The black interior seemed thick and heavy— would he be able to move freely in it? Would his body become stuck inside it like wading through a vat of tar? How deep was it? Tamika, where was she again? She'd be back soon. Not too close to the lashes, a very dark pit of nothingness there, and the inside of this car—who was this person? "Do I know you?"

"Hop in," Lucinda beckoned.

Opaque stared at the lips, how they smiled, and how red they were. Blood? There was something not right—blood, or lipstick? No, he didn't know this person, he'd remember. "Waiting for a friend."

Lucinda shrugged her shoulders in a very male sort of way. Aside from the cosmetics and wardrobe, she wasn't much in the line of femininity. "You could make a new friend."

"No," Opaque said with a confident head shake, "I've got a friend, she's coming here, she's waiting for me...no, I've got a friend, I've got to stay right here. I can't move. Really."

Lucinda nodded. Discouraged, but not dejected. Lucinda was her own woman, flowing with confidence, passionate and alive. "Your loss, sweetie."

Opaque watched the car speed away, trailed by a blur of red lights that seemed to explode from the sickly machine. Red lights, red like her lips, red like blood. "Death rides in that car," Opaque whispered to himself. He was happy that he stood where he stood, firmly planted on the curb of the Drag, waiting for his friend to find him. If he moved, she may never find him...so he stood still, watching the black iron vines that seeped from the soil, twisting amongst one another in a great metal curtain. Yes, a metal curtain that refused to present itself to the hissing stars overhead. Why had he never noticed the stars before?

Saturday, September 19, 1998

11:17am

"Does there come a point when a statue becomes self-aware?" Opaque asked Tamika as they sat on the old concrete steps of the Tamale House #3. A layer of filth separated his legs from the asphalt, the residue from years of spilt salsa, soda, and melted cheese. Permanently stained. He looked to her, watching the last bite of migas slip inside her mouth. "After a piece of marble has been chiseled to represent the shape of a naked Greek man, and all the eyes that look upon it see not a rock but a naked Greek man...does the rock become something greater?"

"I suppose it's still just a rock."

"I think it becomes something more. The power of faith, mixed with our own perception of what we believe things to be...I think that a statue takes on a life of its own. Not that it can think or breathe or move, but it will acquire an aura."

"Maybe." She sat the empty plastic tray aside before relaxing her rotund elbows on bent knees. "Do you think Treva is okay?"

"I thought maybe we could talk about something interesting," Opaque sighed with dramatic exasperation. "Like the aura of rocks."

"I don't think she's okay, she looks really sick. Have you not noticed?"

He turned to her with a crooked face. "Are you kidding? How could I not notice? She's got a foot and two hands in the grave already! That girl is whacked, it doesn't surprise me at all. The nurse must've dropped her on her head."

Tamika laughed lightly.

"I'm not kidding!" he expelled with mock passion. "I've never seen someone so unable to resist temptation. She has no restraint, no discipline. It's pathetic, a real travesty."

"Aren't you the least bit concerned about her?" Tamika asked seriously.

"Oh, yeah...of course I am, but I'm not holding my breath. Who knows what will tickle her fancy next? Whatever she decides, I promise you she'll give in to it. Like I said, no restraint. I've never known a more compulsive person in all my life. Anyway, can we talk about something more interesting? How about the doll, let's talk about its clothes. It needs a new outfit, and that's something that I take very seriously. An improved wardrobe will enhance the aura of anything—even a rock."

She hoisted her hefty frame off the ground and looked out at the constant motion of traffic along Airport. Rain sprinkled from the sky, glistening the road with beads of water that reflected the sparse light of day like imprisoned rainbows. "Shall we start walking back before the rain picks up?"

He stood firmly upright, arching his back as he stretched the full extension of his gangly arms. His burnt orange hair streamed heavenward with black coils twisting through it. It looked like fire. He reached out for her hand, embracing her limp and stubby fingers. Linked together with intertwined knuckles, locked hand in hand, they strolled aimlessly to the road, waiting for a break in traffic. A red light opened a path between idle cars for them to cross to the other side.

"I think Treva's beautiful," Tamika said as they climbed over the train tracks. "And I think she has a great personality. She's always happy, it makes me envious. Makes me wish I knew her better."

"I don't agree," he confessed. "A smile doesn't correlate to a good intention. She smiles because she's insane. Big difference, you know."

"Maybe you're wrong, maybe if you knew her better, you'd decide she's not all that bad."

"I think she's completely selfish," he said with a straight face. "I don't like the way she treats my brother."

"I don't see her as selfish," Tamika challenged.

"I don't see her as anything else."

She thought a moment. "What if she's sick, what would we do? We couldn't take her to a doctor, none of us have any money."

"Sick?" he asked. "She's a junkie...and a whore. And she has my brother by the balls. My brother deserves better company than that."

She shrugged her shoulders in defiance of his statement.

"You don't know him," he told her sharply.

"That's true," she admitted, "I don't. Just like you don't know Treva."

"He's funny," he assured her calmly as he glanced into her deep, dark eyes. Her pupils were lost in the depth of her charcoal eyes. He could faintly see his purple lips smiling in their reflection. "On weekends when we were younger, we'd hang out in malls. He always tried to keep me entertained...he'd go up to strangers and ask what year it was—thinking about it now, I realize how young and stupid we must've been..."

Their pace quickened as the rain once again streamed from the miserably drab sky. They took cover under a weeping willow tree, watching the sky fall upon the saturated earth.

Opaque continued, "as soon as they'd tell him the year, he'd exclaim: My God, the machine worked, Louis is brilliant! Now, to find that android before it's too late." He looked up to see her smile. "Yeah, Jobie was funny. I suppose he still is, he just seems so serious these days." He thought a moment before laughing to himself. "One time, not too long ago, Jobie had this scheme to bring anarchy to Tacoma. He borrowed someone's car, some girl he was messing around with at the time, and at four in the afternoon on Interstate 5 in downtown Tacoma, he straddled two lanes, put the car in Park, locked the keys inside, and just walked off. It was one of the worst days of traffic Tacoma had ever seen."

She giggled with a soft reserve.

"He used to always go to church parking lots, putting stickers on all the fancy cars. Pro-choice, Gay is the Way, Darwin...all the liberal stickers you can think of, and these cars would have their bumpers plastered with them. I can imagine they were on there for months—who looks at their bumpers?"

"Did you like Tacoma?" she asked him.

"I like Austin better. And you? No offense, but my mental image of that town—"

"It really isn't a town," she explained. "It's more a village of trailers, like a super trailer park from hell."

"The community motto being: *We Will Destroy What We Do Not Understand.*"

She laughed. "Yeah, basically. And that was me."

"They never destroyed you," Opaque corrected.

She raised her shoulders in silence as the rain splattered onto the pavement that surrounded them. The tree shrouded them like a green umbrella.

"You obviously had too much character to be a part of the in-crowd," he resolved. "I suppose it's safe to assume you weren't the Homecoming Queen?"

She shook her head with a faint smile.

"I always wanted to be the Homecoming Queen," he admitted. Her smile broadened to laughter, as he knew it would. "Tell me about the best day of your life."

"I don't think I've had it yet," she answered quickly. "The best night, I remember I was supposed to go out with Cindy, and she stood me up, as usual. I was furious, I chased all over everywhere looking for her. I remember feeling so alone that night, I have always been alone...then suddenly I realized as I sat in her gravel drive-way waiting, wondering, worrying...that I was in love. The first time in my life. I can't explain it. But it meant everything to me."

He nodded respectfully.

"Are you ready to go?" she asked with a sudden tone of urgency.

He looked out at the somber neighborhood, through the wetness that made cake of the air. "It's still raining."

"Well," she said before stepping out from under the tree, surrendering to the weather's persistence, "I don't see it stopping. Let's just go." She stood in the downpour watching him shelter himself apprehensively under the hanging leaves.

"But my lovely hair," he groaned. "It'll be ruined."

"Come on, Queen..."

"Does it always rain like this here?" he asked as he stumbled reluctantly into the drizzle.

"No, not at all," she replied. "This is unusual."

They walked several blocks in silence, splashing one another with the water that collected in the cracked asphalt. Opaque's hair fell over his head like an orange hood, a drape over his ghoulishly white face.

"I think Jobie felt responsible for mom leaving," he suddenly revealed to her. "My strongest childhood memories are of Jobie on his bike, riding up and down the streets looking for evidence of her whereabouts. He'd be out there for hours."

"How long has it been since you've seen her?" she asked.

"I don't remember," he murmured. "I don't recall what she even looked like. For all I know, she died back then. To me, she basically did. Not for Jobie, though. He truly believed he could find her, and that she'd take us away from dad. Jobie was obsessed with finding her. He didn't give up for years, and when he did, he gave up on everything. Jobie wasn't always like he is now. Something must've happened when he was a kid, something I don't know about. Our home was not a happy one. Jobie and dad didn't get along at all. I'm so glad we're gone. So glad. I am eager to keep moving, I've never been to New Orleans. I can't wait to get there. But more importantly, my hair is ruined *now*. I'm horrified to be seen in public this way."

"I thought that was what you were shooting for anyway?"

He chuckled to himself, each breath pregnant with pride. "That's quite a compliment, thanks."

"No problem. So what inspired you to look as you do? See, I can look at you and appreciate the effort, I actually admire it quite a bit. But for me to choose to go through such effort every day as you do..."

"In your own way you focus on your physical self every second of the day. You think of what you would like to change about yourself. Well, I actually make those changes daily. The world is a stage and I am the star!" He paused to absorb his own bellowing confidence. "I feel that people seek identity in two

90

different ways. There's the common type who try to meld into the world as part of the flock. These are the people who join social groups, maybe they go to church or are into sports teams that always win, or they are into a style of music that makes them feel part of a unit of something or other. They seek likeness in others, they want to feel that they are normal because they fear not being accepted by the masses, the Average Joes. The far less common types strive for individuality and pride themselves on the unique flavor their existence offers to a bland world. On one hand I really care what people think, yet on the other, I really don't care at all. Does that make sense?"

"Sure. So did you just start dressing odd, or was there some sort of revelation?"

"Ginger Trollop," he said dreamily. "Queen Ginger."

"Was this a band?"

"Nah, it was a friend, I suppose. Then again, more of an inspiration. Met her at Vogues some years ago in Seattle's Capitol Hill. She was about eight years older than me and had been dressing up since she had first laid eyes on Boy George in the eighties. She was elegant and classy and she schooled me on every aspect of the lifestyle. She taught me how to mesh the gender lines and how to shine with dignity and respect. She was my teacher."

"Don't be offended by this, but where does someone who *dresses up* work? How did Queen Ginger earn a living? Drugs? Sex?"

"You'd be surprised. You know the common types I had mentioned—the lemmings? They thirst for me, I break up the patterns in their mundane lives. You know the studio on the Drag where they shoot Austin City Limits? If I waited outside for all the tourists going to the show, I could make a killing just posing for Polaroids with their families. They can show the pictures to friends back in Ohio or wherever to prove they went somewhere exotic, I suppose. People like me belong on the other end of a camera. It's our lot in life. Like I said, you'd be surprised how willing the camera is to find me. I'm an artist, and the art is me. I'm worth a fortune."

5:27pm

Vengeful eyes peered through the dense foliage of shrubs that protected the university from the denizens of the Drag.

Jobie shifted slightly, silently, angling for a better view of the traffic that crawled across the black asphalt of Guadalupe. The world moved ever so slowly around him, unaware of the eyes that preyed in secrecy.

The bruises were slowly fading on his body. His strength was returning. He had even gotten to where he could take a deep breath without feeling the sensation of needles throughout his back, kidneys, and stomach. His limp was also gone.

He took a deep breath of the sticky air that carried the scent of cold rain. Deep purple clouds were clumped on the distant horizon like a pile of grapes. They seemed to be rolling into Travis county with a booming roar of thunder to trumpet their approach.

Across the street on the corner of 22nd sat Dickhead chain-smoking cigarettes. Jobie studied every small detail, all the way down to which of his hands held the cigarette—right hand. Dickhead appeared bored, thoughtless, with his attention focused on a book of matches that he was wasting one by one. He abruptly stood, giving a quick glance to the violet sky before strutting down the Drag to a small gathering of Crusties. A band of Oogles stood nearby, honoring him with a whimsical flare.

Jobie glared, squinting, watching his steps, calculating each movement, formulating assumptions of weakness based solely on the hapless gait of his oblivious subject. He memorized the syncopated rhythm of his walk, the way it sounded like a slow beating heart. There was a casualness to his demeanor, a withdrawn lack of focus that opened up his surroundings. Vulnerable.

The moment was coming.

SATURDAY, SEPTEMBER 26, 1998

The Drag
10:47am

Chasey held out her hand, admiring the way the gold ring looked on her creamy skin. The ring had a faint luster of cream, just a hint of flavor like vanilla. It went well with her complexion.

"Do you want it?" the old woman behind the stand asked with stale charm.

Chasey smiled, never taking her eyes from the shimmering band of gold. "Oh...I suppose not."

"I'm flexible with the price," the woman offered.

"I know, I know," Chasey told her as she slowly, unwillingly removed the ring. She placed it amongst the others that were submerged in a blue velvet showcase. "I just really can't justify it." What she meant was jewelry—especially rings—were ornaments of affection that were given out of love. She had only one ring, the one she received as a gift from her oldest sister years ago. Her jewelry, as sparse as it was, had no memory of men, only family. She'd rather things were different, but her social life never was much. People tended to make her very uncomfortable with their loose attitude on topics she deemed too sacred to even verbalize. Outside the church, she felt she spoke a different language entirely. "Sorry, not today."

"Maybe tomorrow," the woman said to her, familiar with this routine. She felt she should know Chasey on a first name basis by now, with as many times as she came by to admire the rings.

She stepped back from the stand, keeping her blue eyes on the gold ring. "Maybe." Could she find true love in a single day? Maybe what she meant to say was *hopefully*.

Love had been hit and miss in Chasey's life, though mostly miss. She was very active in the church's social circles and singles groups. All of her men were acquired there—she'd have it no other way. Each of the short romances ended with the man's intolerance of her sacred chastity.

Her first true love was a man named Ben. It was her freshman year, and he with his undetermined direction in life was acceptable at that early age. He was an avid rugby player, and Chasey became his eager audience. She never missed a game, owned a home jersey that she cherished too much to wear, and even had a sticker on her car that read *Give Blood, Play Rugby*. Every man thereafter was merely an attempt to recapture that magic she found with him. As with most first loves, she never fully got over him.

Skip was the follow-up, though almost too short a romance to even tally. He was a business major, three years her senior. His indifference was his appeal. She pursued him and his interests with zest, but by the time her first subscription to the Wall Street Journal had arrived, he was already out of her life.

Dusty was a web designer, and the upgraded modem connection she purchased for her computer nearly broke her at the time. Dusty was followed by Ray, the owner of a sporting goods store. In retrospect, she wasn't entirely sure if she was much more than a high-spending regular customer. At the time she saw it as support to her man, but she was left with little more than a closet full of jogging shoes and useless UT paraphernalia like giant orange foam hands extending a stiff index finger.

She roamed through the maze of stands that occupied the empty space between Bevo's bookstore and Texas French Bread. The Renaissance Market. Rows of long tables covered with burgundy and blue cloths displayed the wares of each vendor. Incense, crystals, beads, and jewelry covered the tables, luring the weekend traffic along the Drag. Large canopies hung over the tops of the tables, each a different color like enormous flowers. A mural depicting Texas culture and history covered the outside wall of Texas French Bread.

She would return next weekend, pandering to her own whimsically romantic dreams. The perfect suitor.

She strolled southward down the sidewalk, passing the horseshoe shaped rows of bike racks and the rusted street posts with all the colored fliers. Public announcements, music performances, roommates—one could live by the information posted on these poles.

"Spare some change?" the dull voices beckoned from atop the boxy newspaper stands.

"Sorry," she told them politely. "I can't."

"Bitch," one mumbled under his breath.

Case in point, she thought. Just how disrespectful and undignified our society had become. It appalled her. Her slow and fluid walk mutated into a disturbed stomp as she lumbered to the Bagel Shop. She had just about had it with the Drag. She knew she had long since outgrown her tolerance for the Dragworms.

"May I get a garlic bagel, please?" she asked the young girl behind the counter. "Is the owner Frank here?"

"The *owner*?" the girl asked with a smirk. Her know-it-all expression translated to: *I beg your pardon*? She wrapped the bagel in glossy tissue and passed it across the counter. "You mean the *manager*? Yes, he's out there," she said, pointing to the tall panes of glass.

Chasey looked over her shoulder before sacrificing some change to the metal counter. Outside on the narrow deck was Frank, sitting in solitude, huddling over a piece of paper. She had assumed he was the owner. Why did she feel disappointment in knowing differently?

"He's making the schedule," the girl told her. "He better give me next Saturday off. This is ridiculous working on a Saturday...I could be at Hippie Hollow right now with my friends."

Chasey walked to the side door, onto the deck. "Hello, Frank. Are you busy?"

He looked up with bloodshot eyes that appeared disoriented. His face lit up, and it was clear that he was happy to see her. "No, not at all...have a seat." He quickly cleared room at his table, placing his work in his lap before clasping his hands together over his belly. He let forth a deep and relaxed sigh. "How are you?"

She sat down opposite him and gracefully unwrapped the bagel. "Not too bad. Busy week."

He took a second to cap his fountain pen before forfeiting all his attention to her. "Deadlines?"

"No, although now that you mention it, our self-imposed deadlines aren't very practical. Vaughn is a work-horse."

"Vaughn?"

"Oh," she said quickly, "it's his project, I should've told you that. My boss, basically."

"I see." He wandered into her crystal blue eyes, hoping to retrieve her age or anything else he could excavate. He guessed she was somewhere in her mid-twenties, but he really wasn't sure. She had a style and sophistication that seemed very refined, yet her general physical appearance was quite youthful—deceptively so.

"At times I envy your work," she admitted. "Not that I don't love my research, but there is a constant, on-going issue of ethics involved in my area of study."

"I could see that," he replied casually. His words seemed to open up an awkward silence between them. He sensed a deeper implication hidden in her statement as if she was urging him to strip away her impersonal formalities to unveil a subtle meaning hiding between syllables. Like most women, she seemed to communicate on many levels. As a man, he spoke on a single level—the obvious, blatant one. "Do you feel that this project has an unethical basis?"

"It's not the project itself...maybe I shouldn't say."

"I'm just an ear," he reminded her. "I don't know these people."

She thought a moment as she nibbled on the tough hyde of the bagel. She glanced quickly into his penetrative eyes. Did he find her attractive? "I don't know how to say...do you ever get that feeling in your gut about something or someone or somewhere? Where you feel that someone is a cheat, and you don't know why...or that someplace is dangerous, and you don't know why? It's like God whispering a warning."

"A first impression is the purest insight," he told her as he admired her thick wet lips. "I know that whisper, yes."

She flipped her ponytail off her shoulder, watching as his eyes trailed its descent down her back. "Vaughn presented a report to me early in the week. It's leaps and bounds beyond our best findings. This report—I swear, he has to be testing this rudimentary formula on subjects already. The report lacked any sense of speculation, but that's not what concerns me. It's that he basically demanded four variations of the serum by this weekend, all with levels and properties that we haven't even discussed before. It's essentially the same composition, just that it seems...it seems he now *knows* what effects these combined chemicals are having on the body. It's as if he has moved beyond a rough draft."

Her intelligence both intimidated and intrigued him. Such an educated woman would surely disapprove of his past and all he sacrificed for a buried dream. So impractical. "What is the ethical problem? Should you wait to test this on people? I'm not familiar with the way these things work."

She wondered what kind of living he made as a manager of a bakery. Probably not a whole lot. "Okay, it's probably safe—God knows I can overreact. There's probably nothing to worry about, but when it comes to human testing, there are precautions that need to be addressed and taken very seriously. Large doses of this serum could cause adverse side-effects that we could never have imagined."

Their eyes remained linked, united with desire, though masked with mutual expressions of casual indifference. There was a giddy excitement between them regarding the outcome of unanswered questions pertaining to their compatibility.

"Do you need some type of permit to market genetically altered substances?" he asked.

"Not presently, no," she admitted. "You'd be amazed how many of the foods you eat have been genetically altered. There are no regulations against biological modifications of any kind in this country."

He shook his head in disappointment as his eyes glided over the faint freckles on her nose. "Is there any way you can find out if he is testing it on people? What if you just asked him?"

She could see his eyes roaming about her face, but his thoughts were hidden behind a straight and rigid face. He was the essence of self-control, she thought, yet surely his attentiveness would give some indication. She rubbed her nose to see his response. She was pleased to see his actions unknowingly mirror hers. Yes, she could safely assume that his entire world stretched no farther than her own fair skin. "Of course he'd deny it, and to be realistic, who would he find for this? Honestly, who would submit themselves to such a thing? Seems highly unlikely, and Vaughn is a very respectable and dignified person. I suppose I'm paranoid." She smiled suddenly, falsely. She felt guilty for saying too much, as if she had betrayed Vaughn's name and honor with her petty assumptions. "I'm very driven to do this work, don't get me wrong. I'm just paranoid."

Frank looked into her empty smile as though he was suddenly facing a closed door. He decided to change the subject, tempted by the hopes of unlocking whatever secrets she struggled to contain. "So where are you from?"

"Houston."

Immediately an image of a promising and stale neighborhood flashed in his mind. He found it interesting that that's where her personality seemed most suited. It most certainly wasn't the same for him. "I'm from Kansas."

"Kansas," she said, surprised. "Never known anyone from Kansas. Did you like it there?"

"Not enough to stay there, obviously. Did you like Houston?"

"Sure. Family, you know."

Her response wasn't one he had heard often. Most people he knew were very happy to get away from Houston's faceless sprawl. The city spread like an infection.

"Did you go to college in Kansas?" she asked.

He shook his head, feeling slightly uneasy. He knew his answer would disappoint her. He didn't even want to respond, everything had been going so well. "I've never been to college."

Her eyes widened. His response wasn't one she had heard often. Most everyone she knew had flourished in academics. What on earth had he been thinking?

"Did you go to college here at UT?" he asked.

"I went to graduate school here, but I got my undergraduate at Rice. So did you just decide to move to Austin after high school?" Her question was loaded. She was hoping he'd at least finished high school.

"No, I grew up in a small town, then I moved to Lawrence, Kansas and lived there for about six years before coming here."

He hadn't answered the question she intended, so she tried to be a bit more direct. Simple—the language of men. "Did you like high school?"

"No, I didn't," he said smugly. "In fact, I despised it. How about you?"

"Yes, I enjoyed it. Very much, actually."

He could've guessed as much. She seemed like the type of person who had a good thing to say about everything.

"I've always wanted to live in a small town," she said, "a nice little quaint place where you know your neighbors and everyone's friendly."

He laughed. "That's no small town I've ever seen."

"You didn't like the town, either?"

"No, not at all. I imagine that living in a small town is the closest thing someone can get to the reality of fame. Where everyone knows everything about you except who you really are as a person. They have a stigma of your personality, one that you either earned or inherited, and you never live that down. You will always be whatever makes for the most interesting conversation pieces because all you really are to those people is news. No, I didn't like living in a small town at all."

"You felt judged is what you're saying?" she asked.

His eyes began to wander over her shoulder, out to the street. "In all the wrong ways. I'm not against judgment. I think that the only people who fear judgment are the ones who wouldn't pass it very well. No, I'd want to be judged, personally. I'm a firm believer in judgment, it's the only real way to grow." He looked down at the crucifix that dangled from her neck. "The Catholics were very right about that."

She smiled with delight. "Yes, I agree. I, too, am a firm believer in judgment. I live responsibly and have nothing to hide. Are you Catholic?"

"No. Not at all, actually."

She was becoming frustrated with how his attention was straying from her. Her bright smile revealed nothing of this. "Oh...that's okay. What faith are you?"

"I'm not religious," he said. "Not at all." He could see that she was not satisfied with his answer, so he explained further: "I'm not one to believe that spiritualism is a group effort. I think it's something someone finds on their own or not, and though religion is an adequate vehicle for enlightenment, it's not for everyone."

"I don't agree," she finally snapped as her face straightened. "Christ died for our—"

"I've heard it," he returned swiftly. "I've been pitched before, I believe what I believe—I respect your interests, please respect mine."

"Of course," she said uncomfortably. "Look, I have to go, it's getting late, and I need to meet a friend..."

He considered telling her that lying is a sin in the eyes of her God, but he refrained. "Sure." His tongue held a question, one that he had been prepared to ask, but now seemed perfectly inappropriate. "I'll see you later."

3:33pm

Vaughn scribbled furiously, dictating the results of each combination of the serum on pale green graph paper. The edges of the paper were slightly warped from the humidity that thickened the artificially cool air. The prominent muscles of his forearms flexed with each pen stroke, rippling under the sleeves of his flecked kelly-green shirt. Rubber medical gloves helped to distance himself from his unruly subject, the girl who called herself Purty.

His brow seemed heavy, his eyes narrow with deep concentration. Dark rings from fatigue had settled under his wildly ambitious eyes. His lips were locked together, tense and firm.

The porcelain sink was filled with discarded needles, each one moist with Treva's blood. Her skin was pasty and sweaty with tiny red bumps scaling her body. Her eyes were glazed and wandering. Her head lobbed from shoulder to shoulder as she drooled onto her vomit-stained tank-top.

He dropped the pen to the wooden floor and reached for one of two syringes resting on the edge of the bathtub. A thick orange liquid sloshed inside the narrow tube, clinging to the glass with a gritty film. He tapped the sides of the syringe while he pushed a few drops through the needle, allowing it to ooze down the metal shaft.

He grabbed her limp arm and rammed the needle through her delicate skin just over her wrist. He injected the orange fluid into her body, watching the skin instantly clear itself in a small circle around the point of entry.

"Reaction," he demanded as he glanced down upon his clipboard. "Tell me how it feels."

The room smelled of bodily waste. Her panties were yellowed from urine, and he could only imagine what she was sitting on against the flat wooden chair. He found it hard to even breathe in her presence. He loathed the very thought of her continuing existence.

"How does it feel?" he repeated with agitation. "Does it itch?"

She shook her head slowly.

"No itch at all?" He grabbed her splotchy face with his firm hand, forcing her eyes to recognize his own. Her face was covered with red blistering welts. The saliva that dripped from her scabbed chin dangled onto his firm healthy hand.

"No," she grunted as her eyes roamed back inside her head.

He noted her response quickly before administering the final injection. He tapped the syringe, clearing out the air bubbles as he placed it against one of the more festering blisters on her arm. He shoved it deep into the coarse lesion as a small amount of blood and pus foamed from the injection. The shiny needle penetrated deep into her skin as the white liquid streamed down the shaft of the needle into her bloodstream. Her body heaved violently, over and over, until orange bile spilled from her mouth onto her chest. Her head fell limply to the side as she breathed deeply and uneasily.

"I'll be back in an hour," he announced coldly.

3:34pm

The sign on the door read Jack S. Blanton Museum of Art. Its physical exterior, the Ransom building, was as visually stimulating as a cinder block. It was easy to miss it across from the Baptist church on the Drag. Its creamy walls were textured with the impressions of seashells, giving it the appearance of craters on a lunar landscape.

"I can't believe you've never seen fine art before," Opaque scorned Tamika playfully as they approached the front doors.

"I've seen art."

"I'm not talking about starving artist sales in motel lobbies, I'm talking art that speaks of generations—*fine* art. It's the difference between Pee-Wee baseball and the Major Leagues." He opened the door for her to enter a brand new world of culture, one she hadn't seen before. "You're about to see history."

She led the way through the small entry room, avoiding the smaller displays in glass cases to get to the more spacious interior rooms. The ceilings were tall, and the air was cool, dry, and comfortable. The soft lights washed upon the chalky white walls with numerous paintings drifting through time. Each work

101

spoke of an era, an open window into a portion of history. Directly in front of the main entrance was a sort of shrine, the museum's prize possession—the Gutenberg Bible, one of five existing copies in the United States.

Tamika briefly glanced at the sealed glass display, then continued forward, magnetically drawn to the eruptive instability of a nearby section, the abstract expressionism. The walls were alive with a static explosion of chaos, desperation, and angst.

She hovered over one painting in particular, Joan Mitchell's *Rock Bottom*. She looked closely at it, at the thickness of paint that gave a beveled inconsistency to the work. Under such harsh scrutinized viewing, its flawed human origin was clearly prevalent in the details. The paint seemed scraped and splattered, random and thoughtless. At a distance, it was timeless. "This sums up my life."

"Someday I will make art that will change the world," Opaque resolved with confidence.

Tamika turned to face him with narrowed eyes. She had no idea he harbored artistic motivations. "You paint?"

He laughed. It was a common assumption, though wrong. "No, I sculpt."

"With clay?"

"No, cat shit...what else would I use?" he scoffed as they moved onward through the museum. "Maybe someday I will make a mold of you."

"I don't know about that," she protested. "That amount of clay would cost you a fortune."

He smiled. "Whatever...my creations are abstract, you'd hardly even know it was a person. It'd be angelic. Yeah, you'd be a perfect subject." He paused briefly to examine a work by a man named Soyer. The painting was entitled *Transients*. "Lovely," he sighed with delight. "Such atmosphere, so dark, and yet so human and real. Look at those faces, that's some callused pride. If that expressionist one was you, this one is me."

She stared into the rough detail of the paint's application to affirm its humble hand. It was almost as if she needed proof that someone had in fact taken the time to bring it to life. The human error she sought would only bring her closer to the creator. "I took a photography class in school once. I think that's something I could do...*maybe.*"

They wandered aimlessly, slowly through the maze of separating walls, passing through slivers of time.

"I bet you'd have a good eye for portraits," Opaque said.

"Funny, that was my favorite thing to do—stark portraits in black and white. Like the mood of this one." She focused on a painting called *The Old Model*, "this is what I would try to capture in photographs."

Opaque looked into the withered wisdom of the subject in the painting. Its aged expression was a vault of secrets hidden from the eye of the observer. The lure of it was not to know what the secrets were, but simply to know they were there, safely locked behind the glassy eyes. She would soon be taking them six feet underground.

"That's what I loved about photography," she told him, "the ability to capture the essence of an entire personality with one single picture." She backed away from the painting, deep in thought. "Maybe someday I'll get a camera...I did a photo essay for a class once that I loved. I went to funerals and took pictures of people giving regards to their dead loved ones. I called it *Suffering*. My teacher was appalled." She stopped at an impressionist work, a small painting of a woman wearing a white dress, looking away into the murky gray scenery. "I love this." She glanced at the name, Thomas Eakins' *The Opera Singer*.

"The thing about impressionism is that it's all mood," Opaque commented. "To look upon it for too long is to take away from it. It becomes nothing more than thick, random brushstrokes. It's like a photograph that's horribly out of focus. It's my favorite period of art."

She nodded, never taking her eyes from the painting.

"You do realize that by your own definition, we're wasting our time gawking at canvas that has been ruined with dried, clumpy paint," he noted.

"What do you mean?"

He grabbed her by the arm and pulled her into a nearby section of the museum. He stood her in front of a white marble bust of a woman. "A rock," he told her. "Nothing more."

She smiled.

"This is all that remains of the artist," he said. "This rock, and maybe another one in a different gallery somewhere. The creator of this was named Hiram Powers. In death his name is still spoken. What greater honor is there?"

She looked down at the name of the work. "*Eve Disconsolate.*"

"Someday, when I die, I hope my future artistic creations retire in a place like this. And people can look upon my work and say: *what was this person thinking?* They'll think they know me, but all that really matters is that they know my name."

She thought about how she didn't even *know* his real name. Did he mean for that?

"But we should just leave—why waste our time looking at this rock? You're right," he agreed sarcastically, "we can become no greater than what we were given at birth. That Bible is just paper, and these paintings are old canvas, and this rock..."

"Her hair looks wet," Tamika said of the white marble sculpture, ignoring his biting sarcasm. "No, it *was* wet, and it is now almost dry. Damp. I could dream about her lips." Her own fleshy lips smiled mischievously. "Maybe tonight I will."

"She has wonderful ears," Opaque added. "Does she hear me now?"

"That's not what's important," Tamika replied. "Does Hiram Powers hear his name being spoken?" She slowly angled her head to one side, catching the sparkles of light captured inside the granite. To imagine the bust as a rock was far more difficult than seeing the representation of a woman. Yes, she resolved, it had an aura of life to it. A piece of an artist's soul, still living, even in death.

THURSDAY, OCTOBER 1, 1998

The Drag
10:12pm

The syncopated rhythm of footsteps echoed down 22nd Street. Fallen leaves rose from the blacktop, airborne with the cool wind that howled mercilessly. The air reeked of mulch and grease, aided by a thick humidity that trapped and nurtured the scents of decay. The trees shimmied to the nocturnal breeze, scattering the hard lights of the city across the concrete landscape.

Jobie peered through the black metal bars that held the church like a fortress. He was crouched among the shrubbery, dissolved in darkness, waiting. The footsteps amplified with each step—a single set without a voice. He squeezed the thick tree limb in his hands, feeling its mass, thriving on anger. He had spent many hours that afternoon searching west campus for the perfect stick, heavy and durable.

He looked to the ground, to the shadow that crept along the damp sidewalk. Just as the shadow's legs came into view, Jobie sprang from the darkness with the massive stick raised high over his head. In Dickhead's eyes he saw the horror he had known so well in his life. Before Dickhead could fully raise his arms to defend himself, the piece of wood smacked him across the lips with an explosion of blood and tree bark. Dickhead fell backward to the ground, practically in slow motion, as his hands shrouded his face in pure agonizing pain.

Jobie was quick to return with a second blow, much more calculated than the first. Pulling the stick far back over his head, he smashed it down against Dickhead's ribs with as much strength as he could muster. The impact sent a dull thud through the barren streets. Dickhead curled into a fetal position as his hands covered his face with blood oozing between his fingers, down his arms.

Jobie towered over him in silence, watching his body convulse and flounder, all the while relishing victory. He brought the bulky stick over his opposite shoulder, using his backhand strength to strike another blow to his defenseless head. It was a trick he learned from his dad many years ago, the old backhand finale. The impact seemed to peel away his skin, leaving a nice pinkish-white gouge before the blood surfaced. For that split second, it looked like salmon in a grocery window.

"I told you I'd see you again," Jobie reminded him before he crouched over his body and struck his head once again, peeling the skin, releasing the blood upon the pavement. He tore Dickhead's hands from his bloodied face. He seemed dazed, not completely coherent, yet riddled with fear and confusion. Jobie grabbed both ends of the stick and shoved the blunt end of it directly into Dickhead's nose. There was a loud crackle of bones smashing from the momentum. Blood was everywhere. It made Jobie laugh. He dropped the stick to the bloodstained cement and looked directly upward to the bleak sky, clenching his fists, savoring revenge.

He grabbed Dickhead's arm and dragged him down the sidewalk with strenuous effort and no resistance. Dickhead's feet slid along the cement, scraping the sidewalk like sandpaper with a trail of blood slithering behind them.

A group of young Dragworms were huddled on the corner of 22nd Street. Their menial conversations tapered off as Jobie delivered his prize for all to see. He dropped Dickhead in the middle of them and wiped his bloodied hands on his ripped Crass shirt. He leaned down and searched Dickhead's pockets, finding a couple of dollar bills and the treasure he sought, the butterfly knife. "You guys have a good night," he said as he waved them off before strutting down the street. "I'll see ya 'round."

10:29pm

"I'm just glad I'm not a girl." Opaque popped the lid off the top of his newly acquired black felt pen, allowing it to roll along the sidewalk in front of the Goodall-Wooten. He slowly brought the pen to the doll's lips, painting them black with a steady hand. Its precious nubile eyes peered optimistically up at him, feigning a wicked ferocity. "It's a man's world, sad but true."

Tamika observed his creative efforts over his shoulder, watching as he applied the felt pen to the doll's eyelids, giving it a thick caking of eyeliner. Its pale plastic skin looked morbidly ill in contrast. "I wouldn't necessarily call you a man."

"Not in the conventional sense. Do you see me lugging around tools, keeping tallies on sports? Still, I wouldn't want to be a woman, not in this country. Actually, not in any country." He held up the doll for her to view.

"What are you going to do about the hair?"

He turned the doll around to look into its face. "Leave it as it is?"

"Bald?"

"Sure," he decided spontaneously. "Bald."

"It kind of looks like you," she noted. "Is that intentional?"

"Hmm...more reason to keep it bald, I suppose. There can only be one of me."

"Now let's talk more about your opinion of women," she said. "What's your problem?"

"It's not a problem." He placed the doll in his lap and turned to face her. "It's more empathy. All those expectations, plus the lack of expectation. Were you raised to think you'd ever need to find a career?"

"I wasn't raised to expect much of anything."

"Most of the girls I have known, the thought never crossed their minds. They weren't raised to think that way. They played house, or in other words, their idea of a fun time was pretending they had bills to pay and meals to cook for bitchy little kids. You call that a good time? How can you trust someone who played like that as a child? That's psycho, if you ask me."

"Were you raised to think you'd need to find work someday?" she asked. She put the cap back on the felt marker.

"I suppose so. You know, most boys are asked if they want to grow up to be firemen or cops or astronauts, and all the while they tell the little girls to get used to seeing the kitchen. I mean, is that absurd or what?"

"The hardest part of being female," she figured, "other than monthly cramps, is the emphasis on looks. Not just weight issues, but the idea that women must always smile. If I had a dime for every single time a guy has asked me to smile...but I can't overlook the weight issue. All those magazines everywhere you look."

"That's not men," he corrected. "Those magazines are made for women's interests. Men's magazines show the exact opposite, voluptuous women with big asses. If women stopped buying their trashy magazines, they wouldn't exist. Maybe I'm wrong, but if you think of whose opinion you most fear—is it a man's, or a woman's? When a girl frets about getting a bad reputation, does she really think a guy cares? No, it's the women's opinion that threatens her. Women dress and act as they do because of other women, not because of men. They feel threatened or competitive with one another, it's not always the men who are at fault."

Tamika considered it, nodding. "I can see that. Men aren't innocent, though."

"Neither are women. That's my point. You know, it's perfectly fine for a woman to admit she only wants a man with money, but if a guy says he only wants a woman with large breasts, he's sexist. Now really, what's the difference? Both are typically shallow, yet one is not only accepted, it's considered cute or funny. Why?"

She shrugged her shoulders. "That stuff doesn't apply to me."

"Or me, but in general it's true. Women are taught to receive, men are taught to give."

"Don't date women, then," she said, trying to usher his sexual preference from him.

He smiled without a reply. Instead, he reached inside his brown paper bag and removed a sewing needle with some thick black thread. He lifted the doll to his lap, resting it on his crossed legs.

Tamika watched him sink the needle into the doll's lips, penetrating its fair plastic skin. "I always envied how men could spit," she told him. "Men spit really well. I guess their saliva is thicker, almost like a projectile. Every time I'd try to spit like that, it was like this mist. Never really worked well. I'm not even going to talk about the whole *standing to piss* thing."

"If you could change anything in your life, what would you change?" he asked. "The consistency of your saliva?"

She shrugged her shoulders, thinking of how much she wished she could be the thin glamorous waif that men seemed so driven toward. She knew how well he'd take that answer, though. "What would you change?"

"I'd change my look more often, but I don't have the money at this point in my life. I'm ready for a new look. Now, answer the question. I asked you first."

"I suppose my answer would be the same as yours, I'd change up my looks."

He paused briefly to finish stitching the doll's mouth shut. The black thread crisscrossed over its mouth like a zipper. "You look fine."

"Have you ever fantasized about your own funeral?"

He laughed. "I think everyone does that. Let me guess, really dramatic, tons of people who are painfully miserable to have you gone."

"Really dark and beautiful..."

"I think that's pretty common. People want respect, but moreover I believe we as a species have an overwhelming desire to be remembered after death. Most people pass and are probably forgotten in a year's time. What a curse...that to me would be hell."

Jobie strutted confidently down the sidewalk toward them, smiling with a pompous swagger. He plopped himself next to Opaque, stretching comfortably in the openness of the city's lights.

"Is something wrong?" Opaque asked him. "Why the smile? It's so not you."

He shook his head as he opened the metal butterfly knife. Its blade shimmered in the streetlights. "Everything is great."

Opaque raised a single eyebrow, revealing the elegantly blended colors of blue and purple over his blood-red eyes. He glanced at the unfamiliar new weapon. He had little trouble piecing together the rest of the story. "Do you feel vindicated now?"

Jobie smiled assuredly.

Opaque turned to Tamika. "It needs a leather dress now. I'll have to make it."

Tamika stared down at the doll, at the monstrosity he had produced with such care. It returned the gaze with haunting charisma as the wind chased the leaves down the street.

A shrill scream of a siren echoed in the distance, intensifying by the second. An ambulance turned onto Guadalupe with its red lights blazing throughout the street. Its sound was deafening. It parked on the corner of 22nd, pulling a stretcher from the rear door.

"I wonder what happened," Tamika pondered aloud.

Opaque looked disappointingly at Jobie's smile, exchanging an understanding that went well beyond words.

10:31pm

"These findings are absolutely stunning," Schtepp admitted as he placed Vaughn's report on his desk. It slid easily over the tops of disheveled paperwork. "So how did you come to these conclusions?"

"What conclusions?" Vaughn asked with a very calm reserve.

Schtepp smiled, making a perfectly round sphere of his head. "Don't kid me, you're working with a test subject, I can tell. Who is it? Why didn't you let me know?"

Vaughn shook his head with a devious grin. "I can't lie to you." He picked up the report and quickly thumbed through the pages, allowing it to fan in front of his face. "This is the fruit of my passion. What I have right here in my hands…this would've taken months, and yet here it is. The price for this was nominal, pocket change to a young girl with a bad skin condition."

"Who is she?" Schtepp asked. "Sounds rather sketchy, must you be reminded of the policies—"

"No, I need not," Vaughn interjected quickly, masking his disdain with an even smile. "Would you like to meet her?"

"I would. In fact, I insist."

"This weekend?" Vaughn suggested.

Schtepp grinned shamelessly. The question he had waited to hear for so long, and under these circumstances, his colleague owed him for this breach of trust. Vaughn had no choice, he was suddenly at his mercy, and it was a wondrous feeling. "What time?"

"How does two o'clock Saturday afternoon sound to you?"

"I'll make the time," Schtepp grudgingly replied. "I'll see you then. And this whole procedure better be on the level, otherwise..."

"Trust me," Vaughn ensured him. "Trust me."

3:10am

Bats fluttered over the Congress bridge, visible only for a blink of the eye as they devoured the insects that swarmed under the streetlights. A dense haze thickened the atmosphere, making luminous halos over the artificial lights of the city. Treva glanced back over her shoulder, out the rear window of the Plymouth Fury. Beyond the shark-like fins of the sleek automobile she could see the waters of Town Lake. In the nocturnal shift of days, it looked like a river of black ink flooding the heart of the city.

She wanted to be high again. Her body ached for it. Coming down was hell, and she'd give anything to never have to return ever again.

She turned to face forward, to look out at the enormous state Capitol building at the end of Congress. There was a soft pink luster to it, an attribute of the type of granite used in its construction. Everything is bigger in Texas, and the Capitol was no exception. A perfect replica of the nation's Capitol, though slightly larger.

The electric blue lights from the Franklin Federal building reflected against Phaedra's naturally black hair as Talon steered the Fury down Congress. The street was relatively clear, though not unexpectedly, considering the hour.

There was a shine to Talon's bald head, almost as if it had been polished with wax. The snake tattoo slithered up his spine from beneath his black shirt, resting on the center of his head like a mohawk. Its tail was a rattle, a subtle homage to the state of Texas. Flathead nails pierced his earlobes.

"You're an attractive girl," Phaedra said to Treva as she counted the money that had recently been hers. "You'd earn a lot more money on South Congress than you would bumming change on the Drag."

Treva scowled at her, despising her and her audacious comments. Treva was powerless. She clenched her scaly hands together, feeling the roughness of her skin. She envied Phaedra's perfect complexion. She imagined herself peeling Phaedra's skin off with a knife and wearing it as her own.

"You can earn twenty dollars a blow-job on South Congress," Phaedra suggested as she tucked the money away. She looked after her clients, always quick to suggest more lucrative means of obtaining the steadiest fix. The more they earned, the more she would inevitably earn. "You can suck a lot of dick in one day."

Treva brought her attention to her own arms. The coarse texture of her skin looked like red sand. She hated the fact that she had nothing on Phaedra. She felt revolting and monstrous. It made her desperate for another fix. "How late are you going to be up?" she asked them.

There was no answer.

She thought to herself a moment, realizing that she probably couldn't find the money at this hour anyway. "Where on South Congress?"

"Oltorf," Phaedra told her. "By the grocery store. Walk a couple blocks south, hang out at the bus stop. Someone will pull over, and they won't even care about how you look. They just want their dick sucked."

Treva ran Phaedra's words through her head: *they won't even care about how you look.* Yes, she hated Phaedra. She hated her for every word of truth that tumbled from her beautiful lips.

She covered her scaly arms in shame and pondered how she could get to South Congress on her own. She closed her eyes, savoring the darkness behind her eyelids. She wished herself dead. And why not? She had never truly been alive. She ran her fingers across the cold vinyl of the back seat. She didn't have to look at it to know it was black. She could feel that it was. In her silence, she could hear Talon changing the gears on the push button console as they sat at a red light.

She remembered the darkness of her basement and how mortified by it she was as a child. And yet now she felt so at home in it. She had spent many nights locked in the basement as punishment from her father. She would spend the entire night screaming and crying at the top of the stairs by the locked door, never once looking over her shoulder into the pool of darkness that contained her worst fears. The wooden steps sank into a bleak void that petrified her with fright. Horrific scenes plagued her imagination all throughout the sleepless nights. The fear gnawed on her until sunlight delivered a new day. She was only five years old at the time.

She feared Vaughn in the same way she had feared her father. His eyes contained the darkness of her past. That's why she refused to stop seeing him. Her willingness to participate in his experiment was a triumph of her own withered spirit. Of course, there was also the dilaudid.

Her body hungered for the venom. Her veins seemed empty, just a river of blood lacking the fountain of heaven found in a syringe. In her Eden, she had no fears or insecurities. She, like the rest of the world, was beautiful. Now the lights were out, and there was nothing. No life, no happiness, no reason to live.

She could feel the car turning corners, yanking her frail body from side to side with each change of direction. She felt like a limp doll—a hideous, lifeless doll. When she opened her eyes again, the University Tower peaked over Lavaca. It was bathed in orange light. The mist in the air gave it a majestic presence.

"Get out," Talon breathed softly as he pulled up to the curb on Martin Luther King.

Treva stepped down onto the street and closed the door behind her. They drove off without so much as a single word. She was a ghost to them, the breathing presence of death. Her life meant nothing to them.

As she dragged herself down the lonesome sidewalk, she noticed the black iron fence of the church. Rows of spear-like metal penetrated the earth to repel the evils of the world from its sacred grounds. Each thin shaft of wrought iron dug deeply inside the ground like needles. How she wished it was her arm instead, or her body, for that matter.

She climbed over the low wall of the Bagel Shop's outside deck where Opaque, Tamika, and Jobie were all quietly sleeping on the pebbled surface. She looked down at Jobie, at the stained kilt that fanned over his knobby knees. His legs were hairy and bony with long strips of muscle streaming down his calf under pasty skin.

She curled up next to him, staring at his face and how peaceful and content he appeared while sleeping. She could see the movement of his eyes and wondered what he dreamt. Was it of her? Did anyone other than Jobie dream of her? The web tattoos across his cheeks twitched slightly as she kissed him softly on the forehead. In his arms she felt safe, protected from the world and all the horrors that lurked in the darkness of her youth.

She closed her eyes and smiled. She was asleep within minutes.

SATURDAY, OCTOBER 3, 1998

Quack's on the Drag
11:12am

Frank gazed up from his plate of beans and rice, bringing his attention to two men at a nearby table. He had been listening to their boisterous and pompous conversation, on and off, for the past ten minutes. It was abundantly clear that all of the city's software problems could be cured at the hands of these two long-haired, pony-tailed gentlemen. Frank felt he knew them well, having seen them in so many faces throughout his life. He fabricated the story of their social lives, starting with their early days as rabble-rousers in the user-friendly Heavy Metal scene, then on to the liberation of their college days in the Deadhead scene. It was apparent that they had only recently graduated into Austin's immense pseudo-intellectual scene. Frank figured they would fit in well at Stubb's, incessantly talking their high-tech knowledge, using the word *industry* frequently. There probably wasn't a day that went by where they weren't tuned into KGSR to get an update on what's in vogue in their aloof world.

Frank smirked, finding humor in the way the common majority so desperately seeks a social niche, jumping from one group to the next, never allowing themselves to grow into their own skin but rather a skin they'd like to see themselves wearing. He wondered what these two men saw in the mirror. Did they look into a stranger's eyes? Did they calibrate their happiness by how well they had assimilated into their chosen persona?

Frank took his last bite of beans and rice, ready to return to work when Chasey walked in the front door. He relaxed himself deep in his chair once again as he admired her from afar. He scoffed at her black sweater's satin Jack-O-Lantern stitched on the breast with the words *Happy Halloween* in white comical letters. He wasn't exactly sure what it was about her that moved him. She was typical of what he had come to expect from the world—faceless, lost, and searching—seeking answers in a centuries-old book when the real truth stared at her every morning from her bathroom mirror. To know oneself is to know God, he had always said.

When Chasey noticed Frank sitting at a table in the corner alone, her heart raced. Her emotional response took her aback somewhat. She was really happy to see him, but she wasn't sure why. She didn't even feel comfortable around him, yet it was the source of that discomfort that intrigued her. She sought to understand it. To understand others is to understand oneself, she always said. She smiled at him and waved politely.

Frank wasn't sure how to take the gesture. She would wave to a sworn enemy, he was certain. The truth was so evasive with her that by definition, it didn't even exist. There were merely the trimmings, the color of the wrapping paper. For her, a happy home would be one with an excellent lawn and a shade of paint that accented the lovely flowers that surrounded it. The interior could be rotting with death, a dumping ground for bio-hazardous waste. Face value, nothing more.

They couldn't be more different.

She placed an order for a turkey sandwich and walked directly with it to Frank's table. "May I join you?"

"Of course," he told her as he slouched lazily in his chair.

She formally sat down at the seat facing him, her posture firmly erect. She felt awkwardly stiff in his presence, so she decided to open the conversation with a pessimistic slant to bridge the gap. "I just went to the bank next door, and that manager there is strange."

"First State Bank?"

She nodded. "That woman there, she seems really...inappropriate. I don't like her," she admitted passionately, "she makes me nervous. Her mind is in the gutter, and she makes all these subtle innuendoes about sex." Chasey considered it immoral to even speak of sex, let alone laugh about it. The way she said the word *sex*, it came out like profanity. She suddenly realized that her attempt at snide cynicism had just backfired—she felt more rigid than she did when she arrived. She smiled once again to lighten the air. "So how are you?"

"I'm okay."

"I didn't know you ever left the bagel place," she threw out as humor.

"Have to get away for a little while, even if it's just a block away. The beans and rice here are so cheap, and so good."

"And healthy," she added optimistically.

He nodded in compliance. "Good source of protein. Fuel for my daily swim."

"You swim?"

"At Deep Eddy," he told her flatly, hoping to not go into a discussion about the purity of exercise.

"Good for you," she tweaked positively. She looked into his rugged eyes and smiled. "Got news."

"Really?" He watched her healthy white fingers clutch the turkey sandwich. Her burgundy painted nails looked like the moist skin of plums. She sunk her teeth into the slices of bread, chewing slowly while a single hand covered her closed mouth. She had the most marvelous lips, he noted when she took her hand away. He wanted to kiss her, but more than that, he wanted her to let loose with the vile vocabulary of a trucker. Anything to summon the real human inside.

"So how about this weather?" she asked casually before taking another bite.

"Lots of rain," he mumbled, bored by her small talk.

"I've never known it to rain like this before. It's flooding all over. Have you seen Buda and Kyle? They're underwater. We're witnessing history here, the flood of ninety-eight they'll call it."

"I've seen the news," he said dully, staring deep into her blue eyes, wondering what was the most perverted or sinister thought she had ever conjured. "Quite a thing." He waited patiently for her to finish chewing so she could break whatever news she had.

Her facial expression suddenly fell dour. She leaned forward, edging closer to him. "Yesterday I was sitting on a bench near the corner of 24th and Speedway. I was reading a letter I had gotten in the mail when I saw this young girl pass on the opposite sidewalk. Her skin, let me tell you, she was a fright. I know that sounds rude, and I don't mean to be disrespectful, but she had the most wretched skin condition I have ever seen in my life. I felt pity. I felt for her, whoever she was. And to my shock, she walked to the corner and was picked up by Vaughn."

He wondered what she'd do if he would reach across the table and kiss her passionately. The desire rang with such sincerity because he knew he never would. "Vaughn...the professor?"

She nodded vehemently. "Well, that's all I needed to know. I'm very morally opposed to this apparent arrangement. I feel it's irresponsible and completely unprofessional and it's even deceitful to me as well as Doctor Schtepp. If something happens to that young girl...I'm quitting, Frank. I've decided."

His eyes widened for a moment. "Really?"

"That's the other thing I'm telling you," she began, "I got this letter from a company called GenetiTech, Inc., which is a subsidiary of a larger and older corporation called Hodges, Hull, and Brown Laboratories. I emailed them a few weeks ago, and they called me immediately. They liked my background in both computer and biological sciences, and seemed very eager to have me."

"What would you be doing?"

She hesitated to take another bite. "There is a quest going on right now that you may or may not be aware of, but many universities and private companies are currently working on making a map of the entire human genome, the blueprint of our species. Hodges, Hull, and Brown are one of the leading companies in the race. This will happen within five years, we'll be able to manipulate the chromosomes of our potential offspring to rid them of disease, enhance certain genetic attributes, and so on. That is what GenetiTech has been established to do, to conduct this research. Also, they're working on a software program that will be able to take the DNA of a living organism and by putting its code into the computer, be able to present a three-dimensional image of it. Imagine its use in crime-solving alone. We'd have an immediate picture of the guilty person."

"So you could take the DNA from a sample of hair from a supposed Bigfoot and know immediately whether or not it's some weird unknown species..."

"Or just a bear. Although if we did find something like that, a strand of hair that could prove some cryptozoological mystery, we could produce the creature itself. Instead of us finding it, we'd simply take the data God gave us, and reproduce it in our own labs."

"That's heavy," he replied uneasily. "Almost makes me uncomfortable."

"It shouldn't," she assured him. "Responsibility will accompany such knowledge. If we are to progress any further as a species, we need to accept scientific advancements. There needs to be trust, though."

"Why trust?" he asked.

"Then why not go back to living in caves?"

"I'm not a trusting person," he told her flatly. Could he provoke her to swear? Probably not. He glanced down at her neck lustfully, admiring her transparently soft skin that hid her bluish veins. He wanted desperately to bite her neck, if for any other reason than to tally her response. "Would you have to move for the job?"

"Yes, to Eugene, Oregon. I will leave Austin at the onset of November."

He smiled politely, a bit disheartened for some reason unknown to himself. "Good luck."

*   *   *

1:59pm

Ronald W. Schtepp pulled up to the corner of 51st and Avenue F, yielding cautiously to pedestrians on inline skates as he coasted his sporty white BMW to the side of the curb. He stepped out onto the tarmac that was drowned in a veil of pecan tree leaves. He locked the car, checking it once again for any dents that he may have otherwise missed before climbing inside the vehicle not fifteen minutes earlier.

The brick walkway to Vaughn's front door was a mismatched trail of uneven limestone lined with yellow pansies. The yard was a dark shade of green, thick and healthy from all the rain.

The small house was nowhere near as well kept as his own, in fact, its untidy exterior made him slightly uncomfortable. The lawn was overgrown and rampant with weeds. Fire ant mounds protruded from the grass like zits on an adolescent boy's fuzzy face. The house's white paint was chipped in several locations with its gray and deteriorating wood somewhat visible beneath.

He knocked twice, then a belated third rap for good measure. The door thrust open, and there stood his colleague. He was wearing a green collared shirt with a pair of faded black pants. It was the most casual he had ever seen Vaughn. Then again, it was the first time he had ever seen him outside a professional environment. Schtepp was thrilled to bare witness to this virgin experience.

"Come in, old sport," Vaughn said casually. He held the door as Schtepp stumbled clumsily inside the house. "My home, welcome."

"It's nice," Schtepp stammered submissively.

The interior was far more pleasant than the exterior. The wooden walls seemed to meld into wooden floors, giving the room a very organic feel. Schtepp redecorated the place in his mind, possibly with some English ivy dangling from hanging pots, or even some Ansel Adams photographs to break up the mesmerizing pattern of wood grain.

There came a thumping on the door. The two looked to each other as Vaughn stepped forward to gaze through the side window.

"Ah, she's here," he announced comfortably. He opened the door and in walked Treva dressed in a baby blue summer dress, smelling of cheap perfume. They exchanged a knowing glance before Vaughn turned to Schtepp. "Ronald Schtepp, this is Purty. He's the mastermind."

Schtepp smiled at Treva, though his attention couldn't fully be drawn from the blistering boils that covered her frail, scrawny body. It almost looked as if she had leprosy. "Nice to meet you."

She stared at him with a seething cold glare. This was the doctor behind all this, she presumed. This is the person for whom Richter worked, and this was the person responsible for everything that had happened to her skin. She felt deep anger filter toward him. Her physical deterioration, it was by his rotund hand. Her bloodshot eyes were torched with rage. Her teeth gnashed together.

"I've been working with Purty since mid-September," Vaughn told him loosely. "I'm sorry, Ronald, did you want something to drink?"

"No thanks."

He didn't even think to offer anything to Treva, which Schtepp considered to be rather curious.

"I'm fairly pleased with how things are progressing," Vaughn resolved with confidence. "I anticipate a lot of changes soon. You'll be astounded at my discoveries."

"Can I get a copy of your notes?" Schtepp asked him.

"Of course," he said. "The itch seems to be completely remedied. It's the inflammation that's causing me the grief at this point."

"We may need to resort to conventional means," Schtepp told him casually. "The itch is the biggest problem, of course. We've achieved a milestone with that alone, if your findings prove to be correct."

"Oh, they are as accurate and concise as you'll ever find."

Schtepp smiled proudly. He needn't be told this. He had perfect faith in his colleague. "We're getting there."

Vaughn looked to Treva, who then looked to Schtepp.

"I haven't got a lot of time today," Treva said evenly, as if she was reading lines from a script.

"Oh, I see..." Vaughn replied swiftly. "I guess we'll need to get started. I would ask you to stay, Ronald, but it's not the most exciting practice, as you can well imagine."

"No, I don't mind staying, if you don't mind having me."

Vaughn looked to Treva, sending her another unspoken cue.

"I'd rather it be just Professor Richter." A rumble of hostility shook her words. "If you don't mind..."

"Oh...no, that's fine, that's fine," Schtepp resigned politely. "I suppose I have things to do, I won't keep you."

Vaughn pleasantly escorted him to the door as Treva's eyes tightened with annoyance. Ronald Schtepp, she ran his name over and over in her head. She wouldn't forget it.

"Nice to meet you, Purty," Schtepp said to her before leaving.

She stared evenly at him, mutilating his fat body inside her opulent imagination.

"Goodbye, I'll call you on Monday," Vaughn said as he leaned closer to the door. He resorted to a low whisper. "On the level?"

Schtepp smiled. "Perfectly."

"I figured as much," Vaughn declared confidently before shutting the door. He watched as Schtepp waddled out to his BMW, examining the entire body of the car before getting inside. "That wasn't exactly the most pleasant presentation," he told Treva. He reached inside his pocket and pulled out thirty dollars. He placed it in her hand and said, "You didn't earn this, I can't believe he was convinced of anything...I told you to act civil, and what was all that?"

She shook her head with a posture of fury. "I don't like that guy."

"I don't either," Vaughn told her. "Now get your clothes off and get in the bathroom. We have things to do."

4:10pm

A tremendous roar of car horns and angry screams made chaos of the Drag. The traffic was at a dead stop at 22nd, backed up as far as the eye could see in either direction. It was a curious thing—hundreds of pigeons had suddenly converged upon the intersection, making it impossible to drive without killing them by the dozens. The modern world, in this tiny microcosm, had suddenly halted. The system brought to its knees—not by violence, but by compassion for the living. The Drag was steaming with anger.

Jobie sat on the edge of an empty stone flower box in front of the Bagel Shop, watching the ruckus unfold. He was more than an observer, he was the orchestrator. It was just another experiment to validate the opinions expressed in his writings—that anarchy would not be a difficult thing if the legion of anarchists in the world gave one concentrated effort like this. *The Apolitical Manifesto* sat at his side, awaiting the addition of his latest experiment. He gripped a cup of sesame seeds he had acquired from the Bagel Shop's dumpster, watching the gray pigeons hammer their beaks at the pavement in a feeding frenzy. The birds would need more seed eventually, but for now, it was better to just watch and appreciate.

He dug his fingers inside the cup of sesame seeds, letting the tiny pellets slip between his fingers. A couple of Crusty punk kids wandered in front of him, staring at him with fearful curiosity as they whispered from ear to ear. Jobie had earned an immediate reputation by ridding the streets of Dickhead. He was a force to be reckoned with, and he loved the notoriety. He sat in silence as the Crusties continued onward down the sidewalk, keeping their distance.

He inhaled comfortably, feeling perfectly safe inside his new reputation. He felt such profound confidence knowing that his presence invoked such fear in strangers. If they only knew...

The thought of Treva crossed his mind once again. Every weekend she was nowhere to be found, and never once did she give any indication of her whereabouts. He felt frustration toward her. At times he wished that no one else existed in the world other than the two of them. She was so easily distracted, lured into depravation so easily. If there were no outside influence, she would simply be his.

He thought back to his journey from Los Angeles to San Diego, how they stayed on the beach in Encinitas for three days before heading into downtown San Diego. He recalled a memory that never happened, an event that took place before their introduction. He visualized Treva at his side, sitting on the north shore of Moonlight Beach. Together they watched the setting sun drift under an orange sky. The immense ocean spread before them like grapefruit juice, sending a chilling breeze. Wide open space, safe and alone.

He would take her back there someday.

Tuesday, October 6, 1998

The Drag
5:03pm

His name was Big Sanders. A native of Austin and still living with his grandparents, he was a regular face on the Drag. He was an avid collector of vintage comic books, and would spend weekends playing Magic with a small group of acquaintances at Dragon's Lair comic book shop.

Big Sanders was a bumbling oaf, a large and awkward man in his early twenties, heavy set, but not necessarily obese. He was simply a large person in every respect. His ears on any other man would seem a gross mishap of nature. Thick glasses shielded his squinty eyes that looked like peas lodged in his thick skull. His black T-shirt had the word *Zombie* over a print of some ghastly beast from a campy horror movie.

He stumbled clumsily down the sidewalk of the Drag with a toothy grin of utter bliss pasted across his broad face. A small teenaged girl with bucked-teeth and a non-existent chin clung to his hand, sharing his happiness. Her profile resembled a turtle with no distinction between her neck and jaw.

They giggled through an aimlessly optimistic conversation of no relevance. Happiness spoke clearly through every useless word, defying the restrictions of concrete definitions.

In her eyes, he saw his future. Never before had he seen such a thing. All of his dreams, all of his hopes, materialized in the name of this one girl—Ruth. As they strolled down the street over the heads of the hopeless, he suddenly realized he had never had a happier moment in his life. Never before had he felt so wanted, so comfortable, and so free.

He had spent his life searching for a place, desperate for a sense of belonging. On the Drag, he had found that place. He had friends—he even had stolen the heart of a transient girl to whom he was prepared to devote his entire life. The Drag had given him life, taken him out of his bedroom and away from the comic shops to enter the world of the living. On the Drag he was someone. He was Big Sanders.

Likewise, Ruth had never known love. With a history crooked and shameful enough to boil holy water, she had found her place in his heart. He accepted her and she felt safe with him, protected by his bulldog posturing. It was something she regarded with grave importance based on her helpless past. On the Drag he was someone. She liked that.

His fingers glided along the cold panels of the parked cars as they passed the wrought iron fence that surrounded the Baptist church. Water collected on his immense hand, dripping off his palm.

He barely saw the wiry little body that jumped from behind a parked car. The fist that pulverized his nose wiped the leisure smile off his face. Blood gushed quickly from his flared nostrils as shock immobilized him. His hands rushed to his face as he stared with confusion, trying to understand what had happened. An angry young Crusty punk kid stood in his path with clenched fists and a bent expression. He recognized the webbed tattoos that spanned his hollow cheeks. Purple and yellow bruises covered his face, almost invisible, but still in the final stages of healing. There was rage in this person's eyes, rage like he had never seen before.

"Bad memory?" Jobie hissed. Before he could get a response, he threw a quick fake punch with his left, followed by a hard jab with his right hand straight into Big Sanders' mouth. His head jarred back as Ruth gasped in horror. Jobie threw a firm uppercut to his chin, knocking him back two steps. "Don't remember me?"

Ruth rushed at Jobie with black painted claws reaching for his hardened face. Jobie effortlessly deflected her flailing hands and forced her to the cement, pinning her neck with his duct-taped shoe.

"Stay out of this," Jobie warned her. He looked up at Big Sanders who was now as angry as he was confused. Blood seeped from his mouth and nose, coloring his lips a menacing red. Jobie pulled the butterfly knife out of his pocket, twirling it in a twisting motion that opened the shiny blade.

Big Sanders recognized the knife immediately. Dickhead was his closest friend. He stopped in his tracks, petrified with fear. Ruth curled into a ball, still under Jobie's shoe, with the knife swaying back and forth through the air over her innocent head.

"Please don't hurt him," she sobbed with mercy as tears streamed down her tired face. "Please..."

Jobie tensed his angry eyes that pierced Big Sanders' fleeting sensibility. "Step forward," Jobie insisted.

Big Sanders took a short step closer to the knife with fearful apprehension. There was a wildness to his attacker that he knew wasn't to be trusted. This person could maim him without a second thought, and he had grounds to do so, based on his own memory.

"What is keeping me from digging this knife into your fat gut?" Jobie asked, presenting the question more to himself than to Big Sanders. "I could rip out your entrails and not lose a minute's sleep. I really could. See, I don't give a fuck who you are. You're nothing to me, do you understand?"

Big Sanders nodded.

"Nothing at all," Jobie continued. "And this fucking *whore* of yours...I'd kill her, too. I don't ever want to see either of you down here again. Not while I'm in town. Next time, I'll kill you."

Big Sanders stood quietly as the blood trickled onto his *Zombie* T-shirt. He kept his eye on the shimmering blade.

"Do you remember beating my ass in the alley?" Jobie inquired. "Do you fucking remember pissing on me?"

He nodded regretfully.

"You are a worthless, pathetic coward," Jobie informed him. "Your obedience is blind, you're a big, stupid dog. Today is your lucky day—I'm going to spare you! I'm giving you the respect you never gave me...or yourself. I expect you to return it. Never come near me again. Are we clear on this?"

"Yes."

"Next time I will kill you," Jobie promised sincerely. "Don't think I'm kidding..."

"I can tell you're not."

"Good," Jobie said. "Get your fucking *slut* off the ground, that's no way to treat a lady." He stepped back, allowing them to gather each other in their arms. She was mortified and shaking uncontrollably, babbling like an infant. "Let's not forget this." The raw fear that stifled their movements brought a smile of pride to Jobie's face.

Ruth cried violently as she gurgled indistinguishable noises from deep inside her unhealthy body. Even in Big Sanders' arms, she looked suffocated and trapped. Little did Jobie realize that he was witnessing their final day together. Ruth would be gone in the morning, fleeing Austin forever.

Big Sanders dragged himself shamefully down the street, holding his lover as they carried themselves away from Jobie's domain, the Drag.

5:04pm

"Vaughn," Chasey muttered as he struggled with his green vinyl jacket. She caught him just before he gripped the handle of the office door to leave. "Before you go, I have to tell you something."

He stood at attention, facing her directly with his square and commanding presence.

"I'm moving to Oregon to work for a genetics company."

"Really," he replied evenly without a hint of surprise. "Which company?"

"GenetiTech."

He nodded affirmatively. "Producing good stocks, that company. A wise choice, congratulations."

"My first day is the second of November." She stammered briefly, feeling as though her untimely departure was an act of betrayal. "I, uh...I guess this is my notice. I'm sorry."

"I hate to see you go," he told her without any emotional inflection in his strong voice. "But I wouldn't want to keep you from pursuing a career. We'll discuss it further tomorrow. I'm sure we could renegotiate your contract with the university."

His apathy shook her, though she smiled. Had her involvement in the project really been this futile? All that time spent giving her best to this man, and this was the thank you?

"I'm sorry if I'm leaving you high and dry," she told him politely.

"You're not, we can take over from here, and your efforts have been appreciated." His tone was thick with insincerity. "I'd be more than willing to send you off with a glowing letter of recommendation."

"Thank you," she told him, covering her insult behind a friendly smile.

"Well," he said in a hollow tone, "I must be on my way, things to do."

"Of course," she agreed passively. "We'll talk tomorrow."

11:12pm

Broken glass crushed under the soles of Opaque's lime-green boots. Each creeping step sounded like the crunching of bones. He wearily trailed Tamika through a dark and dismal alley known for its sordid activities. They had been warned against ever going near it, let alone entering. "Why are we here?"

She turned to his ghostly white face, painted up like a Kabuki doll. He practically ran into her. "You know why we're here." Fear and annoyance teetered in her words. She would rather be anywhere else. Yet she lumbered forward into the haze, squinting into the dark crevices between old milk crates and used soda dispensers.

Opaque wrapped his fingers around Tamika's arm, clinging to her for safety. His silver metal claws were cold on her skin. "How do we know she's even out here?" His fiery red eyes peered through the shadows, beyond the torn and dismantled asphalt, searching for Treva amongst the waste. It seemed they were the only living creatures in the entire one-block stretch. That, of course, was what they hoped. "Maybe she's with those people in the black car again. You know how she's always leaving with them."

"Not for this long." She could feel the fear riding up her spine. It didn't help that he walked closer than her own shadow. "I'm worried."

He didn't reply. The sentiment was too obvious to reiterate. He merely stood a step behind her, riding her coattail for support, gripping her arm tightly.

Tamika stopped dead in her tracks with a frightful gasp. She pointed forward to a slender pair of legs stretching out from behind the dumpster. She swallowed hard, fearing the worst.

"If she's dead..." His words trailed into oblivion. He could feel his heart thumping. He grabbed her shoulders, ready to climb up her back.

They cautiously advanced with numbing apprehension. Opaque peered over Tamika's shoulder, hiding behind her for protection. A dark fluid covered the bony legs. It looked like blood.

Tamika's heart raced wildly. She wanted to turn around and run, but she edged closer to the metal dumpster, leaning forward with wide eyes, anticipating the horror. The smell of decay soured the air. It smelled like death.

Holding onto the edges of the cold dumpster, she peeked around the corner, expecting a gruesome mutilation. To her relief, she got neither. It wasn't Treva. It was an Asian man, pantless yet alive, still wearing a polo shirt and a smile. He seemed happy to see them. He was immersed in a putrid stench, covered with a revoltingly foul fluid.

She let out a belated sigh as Opaque glanced safely around her shoulder to bare witness himself.

He had had enough. "This is ridiculous. Let's get out of here." He grabbed Tamika by the arm and continued forward with a brisk and confident pace, leading the way for a change. "She's not here."

Just as his words left his mouth, he spotted Treva's lifeless body. She was curled up on the other side of an industrial-sized air-conditioning unit. She was little more than a contorted ball of human limbs, perfectly immobile.

Her head was awkwardly lodged in the corner between the brick wall and the unit. A hypodermic needle dangled from her arm with streaks of blood dried around the point of injection. Her body was covered with scaly red blemishes that looked like third-degree burns. She barely looked alive.

Tamika rushed to her side, pulling the needle out of her arm and throwing it into the darkness. It ricocheted off the stone wall, falling to the asphalt—ready for another junkie to use. Tamika placed her hand on Treva's prominent ribcage to find a pulse. It was there, faintly.

"Treva," she said desperately. "Get up. Get up, Treva. It's me—it's Tamika. Please wake up."

There was a groveling noise emanating from deep inside her throat. Dried vomit covered her face and neck.

"Treva, wake up!" Opaque demanded fiercely.

She moaned, almost euphorically. The contrasting nature seemed positively evil. The devil was in her.

Tamika gently put Treva's arm over her shoulder and hoisted her from the rubble. She was the weight of a bird. Opaque grabbed her other arm and together they dragged her to the street. The toes of her shoes scraped against the pavement, and her head bobbed from one shoulder to the next. Strings of mucus twirled from her large nostrils. She mumbled disconnected thoughts that seemed torn from her mind in an esoteric collage of utter nonsense. Then came the clearly enunciated: *daddy...hurt me.*

Opaque dreaded Jobie's reaction to the sight of this. He knew Jobie was at the Bagel Shop waiting, worrying. Months ago, he and Opaque had successfully escaped the turmoil of their home, traveled thousands of miles...only for this. The charm of the vagabond lifestyle had lost its luster. He wanted to be home, in his bed, in his known surroundings, comfortable and secure.

"She's dying," Opaque said.

"No," Tamika replied angrily. "That is *not* happening."

Far on the corner, Opaque could see Jobie perched up on the low wall of the Bagel Shop's deck. Even at such a distance, he could sense the hopelessness. When Jobie turned their direction, his eyes livened with charisma. He sprang from the deck, running with tense steps toward them. His fists were drawn into tightened balls, his face hard with eyes that seemed to be melting. He swept Treva up into his arms, tossing her around like a doll as he held her tightly, desperately.

"Where was she?" he asked as he buried his face in her dirty raspberry hair.

Opaque noticed what appeared to be bruises in the shape of someone's hands around her neck. He felt he could almost see the person's fingerprints lodged inside her skin. He backed away from her as Jobie lifted her in his arms, carrying her like a wounded child to the Bagel Shop. He was the unspoken pack leader, protecting his clan.

Tamika and Opaque followed behind him, watching him stagger and sway. Her limbs dangled flaccidly to the ground. Her fingernails scraped the pavement.

Jobie hoisted her over the edge of the outer deck with Opaque's help. Tamika stretched her out onto the pebbled floor as the three of them stood over her sprawled body. Her breathing was shallow, sickly and smelled of death. She looked as if her body had been skinned with only the bloody red muscle visible over brittle bones. Only in death could she weigh less.

Jobie sat in front of her, gently placing her head on his lap. The snot rolled down her hollow cheeks onto his kilt. He caressed her scaly skeletal face, staring longingly into her unresponsive eyes. Her skin seemed charred like a burn victim. The bones of her face protruded under her paper skin, almost ripping through. Her chapped lips were so dry that the cracks were marked with creases of dried blood. Her lips were otherwise white and flushed.

"Treva," Jobie whispered.

"What if she dies?" Opaque murmured hopelessly.

Tamika shot him a hard glance. "She is *not* going to die."

"She's on junk," Opaque told him. "She had a needle in her arm."

Jobie's lips clamped tensely together as his eyes blurred with teardrops. His calm presence crumbled—it wasn't supposed to end like this. He had plans...why hadn't they left town sooner? A tear rolled down his tattooed cheek, falling onto Treva's open and dry mouth. "Please, God..." he mumbled desperately. "Don't do this to me...*please*..."

Treva opened her mouth. Inhuman guttural noises swelled deep from within her throat. "*He...hurt...me.*"

Tamika leaned back against the wall of the narrow deck and slid into the corner. She wrapped her thick arms tightly around her legs and closed her eyes.

She wanted to be anywhere else. All of them wished to be gone, to already be on their way to New Orleans. The air was thick with malcontent.

* * *

2:11am

Chains rattled in the darkness, hidden behind veils of violet tapestries that hung from heaven like mist. The air that surrounded Tamika seemed to glow a deep thickened purple that filled her lungs like grape jelly. Voices whispered, blind scathing voices that were one with the dark, lacking a face or body. Menacing evil whispers.

She lugged forward, stepping through the density with forthright determination. The metal chains faded into the cries of desperation. Human voices, amplified in a ghostly realm.

"Tamika," a familiar voice whispered in her ear.

She was alone, stepping forward. A dark wooden box appeared in the distance, floating in the purple velvet air. Black silhouettes sat morbidly around the box, weeping. The box, she came to realize was a coffin. Her own coffin.

"Tamika," the whisper came once again.

This time she recognized the voice, it was her dead friend Cindy. Upon recognition, Cindy emerged through the coil of darkness. The apparition was a stark representation of her friend, as if she had been recreated with sticks and mud. Its mouth was as hard as a bird's beak. Tamika felt no comfort in her presence. In fact, she was horrified of this demonic beast.

"You promised, Tamika," the thing sobbed. It suddenly looked up at her with a twisted smile that was nothing short of evil. "But you did die, Tamika, you did die."

Tamika shook her head.

The thing nodded in disagreement. "You are dead."

"No, I'm not."

Suddenly the coffin was at her side—a dark shiny wooden box tightly closed.

"You're inside here," the monstrous specter told her. "I wouldn't lie to you."

"You always lied."

The shrieks of pain reverberated through the thick purple air. Cries of desperation. Human voices. Cindy evaporated before her eyes, dispersing into vapor. Tamika was suddenly all alone once again, rid of the presence of the hideous phantom posing as a link to her past.

"She wasn't good for you," a tiny voice rose from the floor.

She looked down to see the doll she had given Opaque. It sat cross-legged, smiling up at her with peaceful, knowing eyes.

"Time to stop running," it told her. Its eyes seemed to dig inside her brain, sweeping the dust from her redundant patterns of thought. "Time to wake up," it said. "Time to wake up."

She opened her eyes quickly, sucking down a deep breath. The doll was next to her, staring her in the eyes, yet perfectly lifeless. She had been dreaming.

A deafening scream of pain shocked her. She looked up to see Jobie and Treva cuddled soundly in the corner, fast asleep. At the opposite end of the narrow deck, Opaque was awake, peeking over the edge of the Bagel Shop's concrete deck. She could sense his fear. It matched her own. Their world, it seemed, was crumbling around them.

She crawled on her hands and knees across the pebbled cement next to him. Painful cries rang from the street corner, no more than twenty feet from where they slept.

"What's going on?" she whispered nervously to Opaque as the horrendously desperate pleas were met only with what sounded like a severe bludgeoning.

"Something bad," he replied softly. "Really bad."

She peeked over the edge of the wall, glimpsing the twisted bodies of several Crusties. They were sprawled on the corner, lying in their own blood, crying in fear and misery. Four mysterious figures with khaki Dockers, black Vans, and black hooded sweatshirts—each with a massive red X stitched on the back, stood over the mess of them, kicking and punching.

"Who are they?" Tamika whispered.

Opaque shook his head in confusion. "A gang?"

"That could've been us sleeping out there," she told him quietly. "We're lucky."

"So far," he replied. "Maybe they know we're here. Maybe we're next."

"Should we wake up Jobie?" she asked.

"He'd be fool enough to try to mix with them," he told her. "Let him sleep."

Tamika sat perfectly still. Her heart raced. "I don't want them to come up here."

"I don't either," Opaque whispered hoarsely.

"I can't deal with this anymore...I can't go to New Orleans," she decided quickly. "I'm sorry."

"Don't be sorry," Opaque mumbled.

"It's not you, I would never back out on you," she assured him. "You're my best friend."

"Trust me, I understand."

Tamika glanced over at Treva's lifeless body as the cries of pain and desperation echoed through the night. Their pleas went unanswered, unnoticed. She could hear the strange visitors walking away, leaving the Crusties in their own pain and misery.

She stared at Treva's wrecked body. It was evident that Jobie held a corpse in his arms.

"I'm changing my life," she told Opaque. "Starting tomorrow."

SATURDAY, OCTOBER 10, 1998

Tamika stood at the register of Urban Outfitters, admiring the ruby red dress that draped over the faux oxidized metal counter. Her dirty pillowcase lay at her side, bulky with keepsakes and coins. She had dedicated every day all week mooching change from sympathetic college students. At the end of each day, she checked up on the dress, making sure it hadn't already been purchased. By the weekend, the dress was not only still on the rack, it had been put on sale. Thirty dollars, a steal.

Tamika lifted her pillowcase onto the counter and lined up thirty stacks of quarters totaling a dollar each. The clerk raised a carefully plucked brow to insinuate the acknowledgement of either a joke or a nuisance. The expression worked both ways.

"Cash in full," Tamika said confidently. Her curly hair was free of the ties, boundless and exploding like a black dandelion.

With grievous exaggerated effort, the clerk scooted the piles of change to the edge of the counter. He released one labored sigh after another as he tore through the shelves, seeking a canister or cup to store all the coins. He rolled his eyes in defeat and left the change piled on the counter, turning his attention to finishing the transaction to be rid of her.

She felt so much joy that she could hardly contain herself. A broad smile of sheer delight radiated from her circular face. "Thank you," she announced proudly as the clerk placed the dress in a paper bag and gave her the receipt. She hoisted the pillowcase over her shoulder and walked to the door. Her hair teetered back and forth, swaying to the rhythm of each step.

The humidity was perfectly visible through the cracked glass of the front door. It made a mess of her frizzy hair.

She concealed her treasure under her arm as she strutted confidently down the Drag to 21st. Her mind was awash with newfound goals and aspirations. She would soon find her own place to live, somewhere in a quiet downtown neighborhood. She'd get a job, she'd take showers every day, sometimes more, if she wanted. That was it, she would be empowered to make her own choices. And after rent was paid, she'd buy another new dress, and eventually she'd buy a stereo and music. She'd buy candles, and eventually a camera. She'd get cornrows. In a matter of months, she'd be truly free. Truly free.

As she reached the massively towering Dobie building, she crossed the street and walked through campus to Speedway. Thunder roared from above, threatening to release the rain that would melt the weightlessness of her hair. The rain fell just as she climbed the steps to the largest dormitory in the United States, Jester Hall.

She walked through its inner corridors, finding her way to the east wing.

"I have an odd favor to ask," she politely told the athletic black man behind the front desk. His orange satin outfit looked like a billboard for Adidas. "I'm homeless, I've been staying on the Drag. I need to find a job, and I'm going to do that today...but I need a shower." She reached inside her pillowcase and grabbed a handful of silver change, mostly nickels and dimes. She held it out in her thick hand. "I'll give you this if you let me use the shower."

He wrinkled his brow, and then shot a quick glance up at her. "You stayin' on the Drag?"

She nodded.

"Damn...that must be hard!"

She smiled. "You ain't kiddin'."

He tensed his lips and shook his head. "Damn...on the Drag...I ain't takin' that money."

"No?"

"Nah...do me no good—go ahead and keep it." He picked up the telephone and quickly dialed a five-digit number. "Get down here," he demanded the person on the other end. "Why? I said so, that's why. Don't worry 'bout it. Get down here. I've got a girl down here, she's wanting to use the shower." He cupped the mouthpiece and held it out from his face. "My girlfriend," he told Tamika. "She talks more than anyone I know." He put the phone back to his thick puckered lips. "Because it'll keep your ass outta confession for a change, doin' a good deed...now how could I take her up there when I'm obviously at the desk—where's your head?" He listened to her talk a while, rolling his eyes, then glancing up at Tamika. "Yeah, she's a sister. All right, then." He hung up the phone. "Damn, that bitch can talk...she'll be down in a minute, after her program ends. She'll take you 'round, get you fixed up, but this is a one-time deal."

"You got it," Tamika sighed with relief.

"Now put that money up before someone takes it...shit."

*   *   *

137

2:32pm

Treva ached for the injection. She fantasized that the needle had become part of her anatomy like a catheter with a constant stream of dilaudid filling her veins. She could no longer tolerate the sight of herself. She cowered from her own grotesque reflection. She had become an abomination, a revolting monstrosity of corrupted flesh.

She fought the desire to cry as Vaughn tied her passive hands to the chair once again. She felt no fear, even at the thought of death. She was already there. Only the needle could bring her life. That's why she returned, that's why she needed him so desperately.

Panic and anger suddenly ripped through her lifeless body. Her teeth gritted together as every muscle clenched. "What have you done to me?"

He squeezed the handkerchief into a knot, confining her for another weekend of testing. He ignored her accusation as he stood behind her, staring down at her filthy hair.

He could feel the arms of failure moving in to embrace him. The serum in all its variations was not working. In fact, it was a catalyst to the problem. At first glance, its application appeared to be a miracle of modern medicine. The results were virtually instantaneous, clearing away the affected area like biological alchemy. Then as the hours passed, the affliction would return with a vengeance, painlessly burning the flesh from within like battery acid. Vaughn was at a loss, and each calculated and educated guess was in vain. His failure greeted him weekly, staring up at him, bound to a wooden chair with hostile eyes. He wished to discard the evidence of his shortcomings, to abolish her existence altogether and work again from scratch. At the rate of her exodermic deterioration, her impending death was unavoidable.

"You made me this way on purpose, didn't you?" she seethed with rage. "You had no desire to help me. You ruined my body for your own little science project, didn't you?"

He looked down upon her with contemptuous eyes that formed a pair of crow's feet. "It's your soul surfacing." He wanted her dead.

Her eyelids narrowed into vengeful slits that revealed the red lesions of skin surrounding her cavernous eye sockets. Her skin had become translucently thin. Her red musculature was almost visible through her disappearing hyde. "I will kill you."

He laughed as he reached to the display of syringes lined across the sink. The contents of each were a mystery to all but him. "How? Here you are bound to this chair, a hostage by your own request, I might add, threatening me. Preposterous! Does anyone even know where you are?"

She stared angrily. Her silence was an adequate response.

"I own you. If you died, no one would know."

"You're wrong," she said quickly. "There is someone out there who knows everything, and he'd kill you."

"Your little boyfriend...isn't that cute? Let me guess, he's on the streets, too? Hmm...what a surprise. What a threat! You can stare at me with all your hate, but you put yourself here, and you continue to do so every weekend...where is my mercy? I have none, to be frank. Oh, but you want this," he said as he shoved a syringe in front of her nose. Its dark fluid swirled inside the casing. "What you live for, that cheap thrill...don't worry, you'll get it."

He lowered it to her arm and shoved the needle into her balmy and pocked skin. He pushed the fluid into her veins, penetrating her body with his fleeting whims and curiosities. He looked into her eyes, seeing her disappointment with retaining her coherence. It wasn't the junk she needed.

"Thought that was it, didn't you?" he taunted. "What if I were to tell you that I just infected you with the AIDS virus? Would you care? Would you even know what just went into your body? Do you care? You are dying, can you not see this?"

"I will kill you," she repeated passionately. She meant every word, too. Once she got her life together. Once the cravings could be curbed by other means.

He laughed at her naiveté. He visualized her body burning to ash with all his missteps in theory vaporizing into nonexistence. Nothing more than a bad memory, bad judgement. "I just might get you first. Sock drawer, it's loaded, I can kill you right now. No one would ever know." He stepped up to the oak medicine cabinets and removed a razor. He placed it in the porcelain sink as he grabbed a handful of her raspberry hair and forced her head back. Her volcanic-colored throat became vulnerable, unprotected from his well-contained rage. He picked up a syringe with his free hand and shoved the needle deep into her neck under her jaw. As his thumb pushed the fluid into her neck, he watched the clouds fall over her eyes as the contents of her stomach spilled from her mouth onto the floor. She smiled blissfully as her head floated atop her shoulders. Bits and pieces of her most recent meal slid from her chin to her neck, clinging to the syringe. "You are the most repulsive being I have ever encountered in my life."

He left the room a moment, returning with a pair of scissors. He grabbed her hair and lifted her face, watching her cough out a giggle from somewhere beyond. He opened the scissors and clasped her hair, cutting away clumps by the handful. Her dirty hair fell to the floor in dark fuscia piles. He then scraped the hair from her scalp with the razor, leaving only the sickly red skin, textured with blood.

"Vanity stripped," he commended himself to an otherwise silent room. He humored the idea of killing her right then, of strangling her to death and taking her body to be dumped in Town Lake later that night. Some random Dragworm, no one would care, including himself. It probably wouldn't even make the papers.

He wrapped his strong hands around her neck as the vomit squished between his fingers. He squeezed tightly, watching her veins thicken from the pressure. Yes, he could kill her, it would be so easy. No one would ever know. He squeezed tighter and tighter until he could feel the air restricting in her lungs. He was overwhelmed with a sense of strength—like nothing he'd ever felt in his life. He could own the hands of death. His body was vibrating with adrenaline, and his otherwise flaccid penis was uncharacteristically erect. He stared passionately into her dilated and bulging eyes. His were ravenous.

He then loosened his grip, watching her head drift to the side. Her breathing returned at a rapid and desperate rate. As he stood over her, watching her, he considered all the ways he could kill her and dispose of her. It'd be so easy. Too easy. He considered slicing her throat, watching the blood flow down her esophagus into her lungs, drowning her on her own lifeline. Of course, he could fill the tub and drown her in the conventional sense. In doing so, he would certainly have to bathe in her blood, just to see what life-giving properties it supposedly had on one's skin. Then there was the gun, although that would only provide the satisfaction of watching her head being ripped apart by the bullet. He would rather her death be administered by his own hands, by his own brutal strength. Therein lied the motivation. Owning the hands of death.

She had nothing to live for, it would be a mercy killing. He would be doing her a favor by ending her life. He thought of how the Nazis had acquired so much medical information by the experiments they performed on the Jews. He found himself in a similar situation with his own experiments, but in this case, no one cared. No one would be busting down his door to save her, she was merely someone else's accident from start to finish. Her only function as a living organism was obviously to be the pawn for a serum that would bare his name, not hers.

He looked down upon her as she sat idly limp, held up only by the fact that she was tied securely to the wooden chair that had become her weekend throne. His work was not quite done. Until then, she still retained a purpose to society. He would kill her, though. Possibly in a week, possibly longer, depending on her value to his research. After which she would be of no further use to the world.

Then he would kill her.

3:56pm

Tamika stepped up to the entrance of the Bagel Shop, dropping her pillowcase between her black loafers. She looked nervously upon the store hours, feeding on the acceleration of her throbbing heart. She was thriving on both anxiety and anticipation. She had spent almost every night in Austin sleeping outside this place, yet now she approached it with different function and meaning. She dug inside her pillowcase, searching for scrunchies to tie her hair into orderly pigtails. She reached to the bottom, fumbling through coins and lint...and a cassette tape. She grabbed the cassette, the only one she had, The Jesus & Mary Chain's *Psychocandy*. So many memories of the life she had once lived, her life before Austin.

She looked up at her reflection in the storefront window. She could hardly recognize the classy image that stood in her place. The red dress shined, she looked marvelous. Her smile was bright and warm and full of self-confidence. Her hair was massive, exploding like lightning in all directions from her head. There were even traces of make-up on her round face.

She looked through the glass beyond her reflection, shocked to realize that she was being watched. A man stood behind the counter, bored, watching her watch herself. It was the manager, Frank. She picked up her pillowcase and walked inside, abandoning her quest for hair ties altogether. She stepped up to the metal counter and relaxed her hands on its cold surface. Smooth jazz filled the air.

"Can I get an application?" she requested politely.

He reached below the counter, staring at her, squinting in an effort to recollect where their paths had crossed. "How do I know you?" He seemed leery of her presence, pestered by a vague and somewhat negative memory. He couldn't place it, though.

She shrugged her shoulders casually. "Hard to say..."

He placed an application on the counter, staring into her dark eyes when suddenly he snapped his fingers. "No, wait, you're one of these kids that hang out on the streets. You're always asleep on the deck every morning when I come in."

She looked at him, then down at the application. Her smile washed away with his realization. She had hoped to begin her new life with a clean slate. She felt like turning around and leaving, giving up entirely on the whole idea.

"Am I wrong?" he asked suspiciously.

"I don't currently have a place to live," she admitted sheepishly. Her eyes shot upward as determination overwhelmed her once again. She clenched her fists on the counter and looked him squarely in the eyes. "Please give me a chance."

"There really aren't a lot of positions..."

"I'll take anything."

He looked at her shaggy hair. It was a frightful mess, though it was clean. That was an improvement, at least. A second glance at her stylish outfit gave room for doubt. She was entirely overdressed, especially for such a laborious job. It did seem out of character for a Dragworm, her behavior. She seemed desperate.

"Where'd you get the dress?" he asked.

"Saved money all week," she responded proudly. "I wanted to make sure that when I went looking for work, the people would know I was serious about it."

He raised his brow, genuinely impressed. "That's a lot of spare change."

"I was determined."

"Where are you from originally?" he questioned. "I mean, when you *did* have a home."

"Kyle, Texas. Where the floods are right now."

"Why do you feel I can trust that you won't be feeding all your friends on the Drag when I'm not here?" he asked.

"I don't have many friends."

"I take it you're trying to get off the streets now? Why?"

She thought a moment, realizing that honesty was probably the best approach. "After my best friend killed herself, I ran away to Austin. I had nothing left, nothing to live for...I don't mean to sound so heavy...it's the truth, though. I think I did the right thing, but out there," she paused to point at the large pane windows, "I've seen a lot of really bad things. I now know where

I don't want to be. I know what I want from life, I know what matters to me."

They stood facing one another without expression. There was a short silence as they determined the size of one another.

"The only shift available is a night baking position," he told her. "That would be to arrive at work at midnight and bake until eight o'clock in the morning. It's not easy. Most people can't handle it. It's not hard to understand why."

"I'll take it," she insisted confidently. "Please. I won't let you down."

He looked straight into her black eyes with a decidedly firm glare. "You better not let me down. I'm giving you only *one* chance—tonight at midnight. One minute late, don't even bother."

She was eager to take him up on his challenge. "I'll be here."

MONDAY, OCTOBER 26, 1998

The Drag
4:46pm

Jobie stared at his brother, needling his red eyes, perturbed. The air between them was icy and dissonant, full of static.

"Not *going*?" Jobie mumbled again to himself. "What do you mean?"

"Just that. I'm staying."

Jobie's eyes squinted hard, tense like his lips. His hands clutched themselves, resistant to the emptiness that now shrouded him like a frozen glove. "How? Why?"

"What do you mean? How...I'll get a job somewhere. Why...we're not traveling, Jobie—we're running. We are so fearful of the past catching us that we haven't a clue as to where we are in life right now. Jobie, we're sleeping on cement every night in the cold. It's only going to get colder, and I know it's only going to get harder. This isn't living. Freedom is control. I need to take *control* of my life."

Jobie was stunned, speechless. He wanted to tell him he couldn't fathom leaving without him, to be on his adventure alone... "Whatever you want."

Opaque nodded. "How will we keep in touch?"

Jobie shook his head with deep dissatisfaction. "That's the deal, now, isn't it? We won't. So the family ends here because you're too fucking scared—"

Opaque laughed sardonically. "I'm not afraid, Jobie, you're the one who is running scared. And you hide behind this Hercules front...give me a month to get a phone, then call me collect from wherever you are. I'll give you my address and all you need to know. I expect to see you on my doorstep at Christmas."

Jobie scowled, grinding the toe of his shoe into the ground.

"This isn't the end, Jobie," Opaque told him. "It's the beginning...it's where our lives start. Who knows what will happen? Might be good, might be bad, but I *know* that now I am holding the wheel. I'll be a free man." He smiled to himself, at the thought.

"Me, too," Jobie scoffed. "I'll be a free man when I drive out of this miserable town *alone*."

"Don't give me that shit, you have Treva."

Jobie bit his lip with a quick nod. "Yeah...yeah."

145

"I'm sorry," Opaque offered. "I can't leave, I can't keep running. You can stay—stay with me. We'll get a place together."

Jobie turned to walk away. "Not a chance." He threw his hand in the air as if to discard his presence entirely. "Not a chance..."

The Bagel Shop
11:47pm

Frank's complexion was ghostly white. He lowered the letter to the table, holding it with shaky hands as the broken streams of streetlights striped the paper with luminescence. His best friend was dying. It was a secret that had been kept from him for years, since they were still in high school back in Iola, Kansas. His friend had been ravaged with rheumatic fever five times in his childhood—none of which Frank ever knew. It had weakened his heart, the doctors didn't expect he'd survive into his twenties. Now they were absolutely certain he wouldn't make it to his thirties. Things had recently turned for the worse.

Frank thought back on all his assumptions of his friend from their past together. He had always thought that his friend lacked the confidence to ever leave Iola to pursue college. Now it was all clear. He was determined to die where he lived, living each day as though his last. Even his friend's wife knew of his declining health. He suddenly felt as if he had never really known him, as if the past they shared was a lie.

There came a gentle tapping at the glass door. He looked up to see Tamika standing with a smile—bright, alert, and ready to bake. She was wearing a thick black shirt and long pink sweatpants. Her hair was teased into a massive afro.

He stood up uneasily to unlock the door. "How are you?"

"Very good, thanks. And you?"

"I've been better," he admitted gravely.

She looked up at him with concern. "Is something wrong?"

"I'd rather not say," he told her abjectly. "Are you ready for another shift?"

She nodded confidently.

"Good, I'm ready to go home."

"How am I doing so far?" she asked.

"Very good, very dependable." There was a lifeless quality to his voice. It was very unlike him.

"Great," she replied, unsure if his mood had anything to do with her.

They walked to the back of the bakery together, stopping in front of the massive silver boiler. The clear water stewed like lava.

"Do you have questions?" he asked.

"None," she replied swiftly.

"You have to be fast at pulling them out of the boiling water," he told her. "That's where you'd lose a lot of time."

"Not a problem. When the morning driver arrives—"

"He'll be in here at five in the morning..."

She smiled. "It will all be done."

His eyes narrowed with uneasiness. "Okay. I'm going to leave...you have my number."

She nodded.

He apprehensively walked to the door. "Call me with any questions."

"I will."

"Okay...goodnight."

She watched him stumble away, groveling in despair. He grabbed a piece of paper from one of the tables and entered the darkness, locking the door behind him.

She glanced up at the bake-list, double-checking her rack of bagel dough. The enormous kettle of water bubbled and steamed to her left as the oven rumbled in front of her with each rack inside rotating like a carnival ride. Blue flames burned brightly behind the racks.

She stepped over to the jambox, fumbling through her pillowcase for music. She grabbed a cassette, the only one she owned—*Psychocandy*. She examined the worn cover, how most of the words had been scratched away from excessive use. She loved this album, though she suddenly realized that she felt nothing toward it, or the past that was intertwined. Those days were gone—in fact, she liked her distance from them. A new day would emerge with the sun at the end of her shift. She was now a creature of the night, hiding from the world, earning an honest living.

She smiled happily as she tossed the cassette in the trash.

*   *   *

11:48pm

"Tell me a story," Treva whispered as she lay at Jobie's side on the Bagel Shop's deck. Her voice was raspy and weak. Her shaved head was no more than a red skull with eyes.

Jobie fell back into reflection, digging deep into his memory. "I caught my dad cheating on my mom once. I was young. I told my mom about it, and the next thing I knew, she was gone. I never saw her again." His voice trembled slightly as he paused to regain some control. "I felt responsible. I felt as though it was my fault. I think my dad felt the same as I did. I don't ever remember getting along with my dad, but I do know that things got much worse after that incident." He turned to face her, resting his cobwebbed cheek against the cold stone surface. "I have never told anyone this, not even my brother."

"That wasn't really a story," she grumbled with disappointment.

"You're right," he said. "That was more of a secret than a story."

"I'm on the inside now, huh?"

"Yeah, you can't say a word." He raised his head from the pebbled cement, looking inside the bakery to catch a glimpse of Tamika working. He felt safer knowing she was in there. He reclined against the hard floor once again. "Let's trade secrets."

"I have no secrets."

"Really?" he challenged. "Then where have you been going every weekend?"

She was silent.

"I want to help you," he told her. "You need to trust me."

She turned her bald head away with disregard. Her scalp was coarse with nicks and scrapes. "I don't need help."

He pulled the butterfly knife from his sporran and placed it in her feeble hand. "I want you to take it, you may need it someday, who knows?"

Her red, scaly fingers glided along the length of it before opening it up to reveal the shiny blade. She squinted as the streetlights ricocheted from the metal into her tired eyes.

"Where have you been going on weekends?" he repeated with a more tenacious tone.

She closed the knife and shoved it inside her deep pocket. "You wouldn't believe me."

"Try me."

"Well," she began as she scratched her enflamed and hairless head with her fingernails. Droplets of blood surfaced on her dry scalp, following a trail from her dirty nails. "I've been getting help from a doctor. He's been looking at my skin." Even as the words escaped her mouth, she knew it sounded absurd. It was apparent that her health had worsened progressively with each visit.

He was somewhat startled, expecting anything but the truth. Was this just a strange affliction that would soon be cured? He could only hope, for his hormone's sake.

Suddenly she burst into tears. "I'm dying..." she sobbed. "And I'm hideous."

His face briefly lit with an empowering smile. Her weakened spirit harmonized with his insurmountable interest. The deeper she slid into despair, the closer he felt to her. "No, you're not."

"Yes, I am. I don't know what he's done to me...and now I can't stop seeing him..."

"Why?"

"Because he's supposed to be curing it. And the money...I need money."

"What money?" The desperation in her voice irritated him. Her submissive dependence infuriated him further. "He pays you?"

"Yes," she replied with a passive sniffle.

"Is he rich?"

"I don't know..."

His face clenched with anger. He felt insecurity about her reliance upon this person's charity. It enraged him to know that a stranger offered something to her that he never could. "I hate rich people. I want you to stop seeing him."

She silently wept. "I can't."

"Why? Is he the person who cut off your hair? I thought you loved your hair..."

"Leave me alone," she replied angrily.

His eyes tightened with hostility. "Where does he live? Are you fucking him?"

"No, and if I was, it's not your business." She sat upright, leveraging herself with her palms. She felt weak and dizzy. Her head seemed to be floating over her shoulders, practically blind and numb to her surroundings.

"It *is* my business," he concluded aggressively. "*You* are my business. Do you not realize what I have done for you?"

The truth of his statement besieged her with guilt. "You've done nothing. You think I need you?"

He remained still, deflecting the threat with silence.

"I won't stop seeing him," she insisted. "Not until my skin is normal."

"You honestly believe he will cure you?"

She knew he wouldn't, or it would already have been done. "Yes," she belied hastily, deceiving only herself.

"You make it very hard to give a shit about you," he admitted. "You depend on all these people, but who are they? They control your life."

"Shut up," she hissed. Again, the truth was too venomous for her to handle. She imagined the needle penetrating her skin, sending her far away. That's all she really wanted. "You don't know."

"I think I *do* know—I know better than you do."

She thought a while, maintaining an awkward silence. When she spoke again, her voice was as soft as a child's. "Let's leave Austin. Let's go to New Orleans. Let's go tonight."

"You're too sick to leave."

"I'm not either," she declared with a recognizable exhaustion. "I'm ready to go, I'm ready now. Let's do it, let's leave."

"Not yet."

She scoffed aloud. "I need to go, there's nothing more I want than that. Please, Jobie, let's leave town tonight—*right now.*"

"You need to sever all your ties here, at whatever cost," he told her. "*At whatever cost.* Trust me, I want to leave as badly as you do. I want it so badly I can taste it. In fact, I can't think of anything I want more. I can feel the walls of this town closing in on me, I see it in the way these people look at me. They want me dead, but they're too afraid to even look at me..."

"All that we need to do to leave is to stand up and start walking. We can leave all this behind us right now. It'd be just you and me. You and me."

The idea of it wasn't short of appeal. He weighed the possibilities before realizing how futile it was to even consider. It frustrated him how unaware she seemed of the circumstances. Her circumstances became his burden, and he begrudged her for it. "Not until you get well again."

She sat quietly a moment, thinking to herself. The thought of everyone she had met in Austin filled her with resentment. "I'll get them out of my life." Her rage simmered inside her, waiting to explode. "I know what I'm going to do. I will need your help."

He sat up, eager to listen, eager to help. "Let's hear it."

She laid out her plan in all its brutality. As she had suspected, he was willing to participate in her nefarious scheme. They immediately began plotting the details of her revenge.

SATURDAY, OCTOBER 31, 1998

Sixth Street
10:17pm

Chasey edged her way down Sixth Street alone, admiring the elaborate costumes of the thousands who packed the notoriously renowned spectacle. It was her last night in Austin. Halloween. She would have preferred to spend it with anyone other than only herself, but her options were few and far between. She hoped that a higher level of morality existed where she was going, because Austin had proven itself to be nothing more than a thoroughfare for marauders and sinners.

A couple passed—the male wearing a crown of thorns with a white robe, while the female was clearly the Virgin Mary.

"Forgive them for their sins, Father," she whispered under her breath. "They mock you in vain, forgive them."

No, she wouldn't be missing much by leaving this town. She would be leaving as she arrived, hopeful and empty-handed.

Her attention quickly strayed to a young couple standing on the curb watching the mob of ghouls and hooligans flaunt their pageantry. She recognized the young girl, her horrendous skin infliction made her stand out as one of the most hideous monsters on the street. On a night like this she would mix well with the crowd, just another vile island in a sea of atrocity.

"Have mercy on her," Chasey whispered to the cool air that blew through the crowded streets. She turned to walk down a side street with one last glimpse of the wild extravaganza she would soon be leaving behind. "Goodbye, Austin."

10:32pm

The black Fury drifted through a veil of fog down a vacant alley. The headlights sliced the haze of cold humidity as its rubber tires splashed through potholes of stagnant water. The brick walls were glazed with a slippery sheen from all the rain. The city was waterlogged.

Phaedra glanced into the rearview mirror, into her own reflection. Her almond-shaped eyes looked upon themselves with deep satisfaction. Her black hair was clean and straight, shining like her latex corset and skirt. It made her soft skin seem pale in contrast. She was looking her best, ready for the

153

performance of the year, the annual S&M Ball at the Voodoo Lounge. She was to be on stage within the hour, submitting her flesh to the whip.

Her savagely beautiful eyes caught sight of Treva standing by the alleyway entrance to the Voodoo Lounge. Early as expected. When Treva turned to face the Fury, Phaedra gasped. Her skin appeared to be melting off her malnourished muscles and bones. Her face looked like a skull covered in red wax with shifty, volatile eyes. She had the eyes of death, as though her life had been stripped, leaving only a mobile skeletal corpse in its place. Her clothes draped her bony frame as if to mock her rapid decline. They were designed to accent the body, not flaunt its deterioration. She was a walking disease.

She nudged forward with the grace and fluidity of an insect as the Fury rolled to a stop. She perched her weight on the car's black hood to support her languid body. Her flesh began to burn with envy as Phaedra's beauty ate her like cancer. She missed her own haystack hair. In fact, there wasn't much she didn't miss, including her sanity. "Do you have it?" Her voice was raspy and weak.

Phaedra opened the car door, leaving the engine running with the headlights ablaze. She placed her latex knee-high boot onto the sticky blacktop, standing upright from the driver seat. She held the leather pouch in her smooth hands. "Money?"

Treva hunched over the hood, barely holding herself vertical as she tilted her ghastly head to seek the darkness. "Away from sight."

Jobie stood at the end of the alley, secretly watching the exchange through a blanket of fog. He scanned Trinity to the police barricades at Fifth, relishing the macabre atmosphere of Austin's traditional Halloween celebration. Superheroes and legendary monsters emerged from back streets, filing into the herd that revolved in a massive circle up and down Sixth. Loud music sprang from every bar along the old street, meshing into a thick fuzzy noise of sporadic rhythms. It sounded better as one conglomerate mess, a hodgepodge of American pop culture in all its faceless glory.

He watched Treva hobble to the dark space behind the dumpster. Phaedra followed a few steps behind as though she were pacing herself with an elderly woman. Treva turned to her, just out of the way of the Fury's headlights. No one was around.

"Let's make this fast," Phaedra demanded. Her tight black latex outfit stretched provocatively over her supple skin. It devoured light like a black hole. It made Treva furious. "I need to meet Talon right now." She looked at the scabs that covered

Treva's poorly shaved scalp. She made a foul face of repulsion. "You look like rotting hamburger meat."

Treva didn't reply. Instead, she mentally carved the flesh off Phaedra's flawless body. Her mind was a scrambled mess of fantastical murder and mutilation—it brought a warm smile to her wretched face, only to fade into a hateful scowl. She could barely focus her thoughts over the muddled sounds of digitized music throbbing in the distance on Sixth Street. She looked down at the lethal hand that served her death in a syringe. She wanted to skin her alive. Given the opportunity, she'd do it, too.

"Where's the money?" Phaedra repeated.

Treva reached into her back pocket as she glanced down the alley through the rolling fog. She gripped the cold metal butterfly knife in her hand, opening it inside her deep pocket. She could feel the blade's length in her pants as it became fully extended, yet hidden from view. Just as Phaedra's attention went to her leather pouch, Treva lunged forward, thrusting the blade inside her chest. She felt it cracking through bone and cartilage before piercing the softer organs.

Phaedra's beautiful eyes widened with horror, unable to even react defensively. She instinctively grabbed at the knife, clasping onto Treva's grotesquely scaly hand. No words or noises escaped her mouth, only panic melting the transparent beauty of her face. Treva covered Phaedra's gaping mouth with a cold, claw-like hand while slowly pushing her back against the moist brick. The blood trickled down the black latex, over her bronzed muscular legs, to the beer-stained ground. Before there could be a struggle, it was over. Phaedra slid down the wall to the blacktop, dead. Her body twitched.

Treva smiled with wild excitement as footsteps raced down the alley toward her.

Jobie rushed to Treva's side, staring at the bloody body that stared back like a wax mannequin. He shook his head, smiling. "Ain't nothing but a damn thing."

Treva trembled with delight. She fell to her knees, running her fingers through the blood that seeped from the wound. She brought her fingers to her mouth, licking them clean. She rubbed her victim's blood on her own hollow cheeks, painting her face with fresh death. She was alive once again.

"Come on," Jobie demanded uneasily as he pulled Treva away from the bloody body. "Let's get her out of here."

He reached down and lifted Phaedra's limp body, leaving the knife deep inside her chest. He dragged her back to the Fury, opening the passenger door just as the alleyway entrance of the Voodoo Lounge opened. Jobie dropped Phaedra to the pavement as three costumed gladiators stopped to witness.

"Holy shit, that looks real," one said excitedly.

"Totally," the other replied. "You should've had the bartender cut her off an hour ago." He glanced at Treva's skin, how it seemed to be dripping off her body. "You guys should work in Hollywood...except those tattoos on your face, they don't look real at all. No one tattoos their face." They continued onward to Sixth Street, seeking more costumes and facades to criticize.

Jobie lifted Phaedra into the car, shoving her limp and bloody body into the backseat.

The black Fury disappeared into the dark haze.

11:59pm

Treva dragged the corpse from the car, pulling it through the dark open country. The sky was a dull pink from the nearby city lights, and the air was alive with the strident sounds of cars racing down the Capital of Texas highway. She propped the body up on a rock as Jobie stood at her side drinking Everclear from the bottle.

"Purty," she said to him as she coddled the dead body like an infant. A cigarette burned in her chapped lips. "That's her name. Her name is Purty, the little cock-socket slut."

Jobie took a quick gulp to squelch his thoughts. The alcohol burned his throat like petrol. He was eager to leave Austin. It was coming so soon, he could taste it. He wanted nothing more than to stare out at a dark and lonely highway facing an open future. He watched Treva strip the corpse of its stylish clothes, setting them in a neat pile at her side. The corpse's head lolled to its shoulder.

"Shut up, Purty," Treva lambasted the corpse as though it had smarted off. "No one wants to hear you talk. You're just pussy." She caressed the corpse's breasts with her fulsome hands, pinching its nipples. She ran her hands down its smooth stomach over the leopard spot tattoos. She spread the corpse's legs, airing its shaved genitalia. The labia were pierced in several places with silver barbells tapering from the hood of the clitoris. Treva shoved a finger inside its vagina as she said, "You're a whore, Purty...you're a fucking whore." Her childish voice was exacerbated. "No one likes you when your legs are closed."

"Treeeva," Jobie slurred with a kowtow, "maybe you need...a drink." He held out his bottle to her. "We need to get ridda this fuggin' body."

"I want to keep it," she insisted as she grabbed the bottle and took a sip. She exhaled the fumes with a gasp. "It's me. She's mine because now she's me. I want to keep her." She poured the contents of the bottle all over the corpse, dousing its black hair, covering its shapely body with the stench of alcohol. Treva hugged the corpse tightly, affectionately.

Jobie rolled his eyes, mildly humored by her daftly capricious behavior.

Treva dropped her cigarette into its lap and watched it smolder. No effect. She took out her lighter and lit its hair on fire. The alcohol caught the fire and pulled it down over the body like a shroud. The flames ate at the skin, blanching it before it flowered into a shade of damask.

The pupils of Jobie's eyes receded in the heat as he watched Treva slink and careen around the body, giggling as the beauty of the corpse boiled hairless. He only wished she hadn't wasted all his liquor on this crazed spectacle. The flames dispersed as quickly as they spread, leaving its skin covered with red abrasions and boils. It bore a stark resemblance to Treva.

"Isn't she pretty?" she asked him. "See, she's me now."

"Yeah," he mumbled nonchalantly. There was an irrefutable similarity. "She's pretty, all right."

"She's me," Treva declared with sheer delight. "Do you want to touch her pussy before I skin her?"

MONDAY, NOVEMBER 2, 1998

Hyde Park
2:10pm

Sunlight streamed through the open window, following a refreshingly dry breeze. The sky was vast and open, a solid shade of clear blue with tumbling white clouds sparsely spanning the horizons. The saturated land was suddenly alive once again. The world shined green.

Tamika sat in the center of her bare studio apartment, savoring the tranquility of an easy afternoon. The sunlight covered her body, warming her mocha skin with its surplus of vitality. On the floor next to her was the twelve-month lease for her new efficiency. Her bold signature was scratched at the bottom of the lengthy contract.

She hadn't budged an inch in hours. There was no place to be and nothing to do other than what she was already doing. Of course, she could run down to the nearby Fresh Plus grocery to stop the growling in her stomach, but that would require so much effort...

She had taken the time earlier in the day to absorb her new surroundings. She had stared at the walls, correlating the glossy sheen of the creamy paint with tasty peach pudding. She familiarized herself with the ceiling's bumpy white buttermilk texture. Silver glitter clung to its surface for some sort of starry effect when struck with light. The carpet on which she reclined was soft and gray. Stone gray. Much like the sky had been. The door was the same color as the walls, easy for it to disappear if not for the bronze doorknob. In its reflection she could see herself lounging in an empty room. Her room.

In the corner of the efficiency was her pillowcase with all her clothing spilling onto the floor. Her new red dress had the contrasting luminosity of a fiery Phoenix rising from the ashen carpet. One picture hung from the glossy wall, her own Christmas picture from years ago. She finally recognized that giddy smile. It was her own.

A gentle rapping came to the door.

She rose to her feet, excited to receive her first guest. She was stiff from immobility. It was a nice feeling, one she hadn't felt enough of lately.

Opaque stood in the doorway, his black lips grinning as he held his morose doll like a docile infant. His dour facial paint didn't mix well with the brightness of the day. The straps that connected his black bondage pants seemed restrictive, and his

159

black chiffon shirt was a bit too snug for comfort. He seemed stiff and colorless, contrary to his trademark regality. The pink crepe myrtles along the street easily stole his limelight.

"Come in," she beckoned hospitably.

He entered with rigid steps, slightly uncomfortable with what seemed a formality, as he browsed the room. He felt like a stranger. Moreover, he felt like the train had left without him, leaving him alone on an empty avenue without many options. "Nice."

She closed the door behind him, trapping them both inside the comfortable little shell. She teased her frayed hair into a relatively presentable shape. Her gestures were free and easy, naturally uninhibited by his presence. "Do you really like it?"

"I do."

"It was cheap," she said. "I'll be able to afford it without any problem."

He walked over to the one picture on the wall. "That's you."

"Yes, it is." She dropped herself back on the carpet in the center of the unfurnished room. "Please sit down, relax...my place is yours."

He did as she requested, sliding down the wall, stretching his legs across the floor. "I love the Victorians in this neighborhood. Someday I want to live in one."

"Hyde Park," she said. "Gotta love it. The yards out here are like art. All the flowers, the trees, the new paint on the old houses...the apartments aren't quite up to scale, though. An eyesore, really, in a neighborhood like this. Students. All their balconies are used as a storage space for odds and ends. It wouldn't be hard to fill this tiny space, though."

"You can almost get a sense of your neighbors just by the contents of their balconies."

She nodded. "Bikes they never use."

"This is great," he suddenly exclaimed, capturing his sudden realization. "Your own apartment. How vogue you are now."

"No more sleeping on the Drag," she gloated. "I'm going to buy a bed with my next paycheck. Do you want to have a slumber party when I get it?"

"If you fall asleep, you know I'll put your fingers in warm water so you'll piss yourself."

"Any time you want," she told him seriously, "the place is yours."

"Watch your offers...I'll become a nuisance really fast."

"No," she said quite simply, "trust me, I know—I wouldn't go back to that pavement for another second. Speaking of, have you talked with Jobie and Treva about leaving for New Orleans?"

"I have no idea where they are. Haven't seen them in days."

"Let me ask you a question," she proposed uneasily. "You may decline, but I must ask. How would you feel about being my roommate? I mean, we could buy twin beds—the place is small, but the rent is cheap, we'd pull ahead in no time. You'd be off the streets, too. I will worry about you now, you know."

He looked up at her, linking the gaze of his red eyes with her deeply sensitive black eyes. There existed a mutual depth of understanding between them. More so than even she knew. "I would love to."

"Really?"

"Yes. We could save money and travel in style, no jumping cargo trains, or sleeping on the streets...we could sleep in motels if we chose to travel again."

She smiled gleefully like a child. Like the photograph on the wall. "I'm so happy to hear that."

"I'm so happy you asked," he admitted, "and I promise I'll find work so that I can keep up my end of rent. Hell, if I have to cut my hair and go New Romantic, then I will." His stiff posture became elastic. "Where would my bed go?"

"Wherever you want," she replied. "It'd be your place, too."

He studied the room, gauging the amount of space he'd require, which wasn't much. Though it was small and boxy and would inevitably be far too cramped for two people to share for very long, its potential for freedom was immense and boundless.

"Do you mind if I take a shower *right now?*" he pleaded. "I can't even remember how long it's been."

"It's your place," she reminded him. She really liked that, the sound of her own generosity. It was nice to finally have something to offer. "Have at it."

He stood eagerly, rushing into the bathroom that was roughly the size of a walk-in closet. He shut the door, closing off the entire world. There was a sense of privacy he hadn't felt since he left Washington. He twisted the plastic knobs of the faucet and watched the water swirl down the drain. The rest of his afternoon disappeared with it as the clock ticked in the company of deaf ears. The air-conditioner exhaled its pleasantly cool breath upon him, relaxing his hardened senses as he focused on the sound of water, allowing his mind to drift to thoughtlessness. He collapsed to the floor without a care in the world. It was one of the most exciting moments of his life.

Tamika was almost asleep by the time he had actually bathed. She rubbed her tired eyes with thick knuckles, only to open them to an unfamiliar young man wrapped in a towel. His lips were a nice skin-tone, and his eyes were a warm shade of brown. She never knew. His skin was clean and cosmetic-free—

he looked very male, and quite attractive. His orange and black hair was clean and slicked back over his well-sculpted head.

"True euphoria," he remarked on his showering experience. His voice was calm and mellow, gruff and gravelly. "I feel like a new woman."

Her lips stretched briefly into a smile as she remained fixed on the face of a friend she had never actually seen before. Why had she never acknowledged this mask?

He was quick to realize her thoughts through her awe-struck expression. "My real name is Rik," he told her. "Rik Wallace. Have I ever told you that?"

She shook her head, comforting herself with his unexpected handsome masculinity. It was the most extreme change she had yet seen with him.

"Nice to meet you, Rik," she told him sarcastically. "Are you hungry? I'm famished. I have some extra money from my paycheck, maybe we should order a pizza..."

He laughed as he took a seat by the door, sprawling comfortably on the floor. "We don't have a phone."

"We'll have to put that on the list of things to get...a phone...to order pizzas." She looked up at him and smiled. "I'm so glad you're here."

He inhaled deeply, followed with a rich sigh of relief. "Glad to be here. I have a home again." He closed his eyes, basking in the serenity. His face was strong and firm, perfectly male. Their genders had suddenly split from one another for the very first time. "Home," he murmured before falling into a deep and peaceful slumber. It was almost as though he had never used the word.

2:11pm

Jobie savored the rush of attention that unwittingly tended him from across Sound Exchange. His eyes remained low, seemingly focused on the stacks of seven-inch vinyl records in the sale bin, flipping through them with dirty fingers. His presence was calm and unimposing, though the overbearing sense of caution amplified his blood pressure like a drum. His peripheral vision kept the observers in check—two Oogles who had been trailing him for over an hour. Inconspicuously so, but not in Jobie's eyes—he was very aware of them. A brief glance revealed their interest was not fueled by respect. Dickhead loyalists, typical Oogles vying for acceptance in the dregs, begging to have a semblance of an identity as lowly disheveled vagabonds.

Jobie pulled out a record of a band called Lower Class Brats and brought it to the counter. As he stood before the cash register, he felt the presence of the two Oogles closing in on him. The hardcore music that played throughout the store put him somewhat at ease as another confrontation seemed imminent. It had been so long since he had heard *good* music— it was just the boost he needed. To him, the greatest invention of mankind wasn't the wheel, it was music. Hardcore music, specifically. Fuel for the fire.

Without saying a word, he placed the exact change on the counter and walked outside into the dimming light of day. As he passed around the corner of 21st, he caught sight of the two Oogles following relatively close behind with hard, rugged steps. He walked calmly to the alley, away from the safety of the public eye. The butterfly knife, his only weapon, was in the possession of Treva—he was defenseless.

He pulled the record from the sleeve, focusing on the circular grooves in the black vinyl before breaking it into two serrated pieces.

As he turned the corner to walk into the alley, he slipped behind the wall with his lethal shard of vinyl poised in his hand, waiting to strike. Within seconds, he could hear the kicking of rocks from aggravated steps as they rounded the corner. He sprang from behind the wall, thrusting the jagged vinyl into the throat of his nearest opponent. It penetrated the flesh beneath his chin with a gush of blood streaming down the black vinyl. The broken piece of record dangled from his chin before he pulled it free in a panic. It let loose the flow of blood as though a cork had been popped.

Jobie grabbed the clean Misfits T-shirt of the other Oogle and shoved him backward against the brick wall. His shoulders impacted with a dull thud that loosened the corner bricks of the crumbling wall. Jobie held him tightly by the collar, staring wildly into his eyes with biting anger. He kneed him in the groin and pulled him to the ground amongst the rubble, pinning him with his foot. Jobie stood over him, staring down at his unknown opponent as his crony gripped his own bleeding neck, wandering in frantic circles. Jobie picked up one of the loosened bricks and smacked it over the downed Oogle's head, leaving him limp and still.

"What do you want?" Jobie asked his bleeding comrade.

The Oogle stared with wide eyes that swelled with tears.

"You fucking coward," Jobie told him as he stood toe to toe. "You want me to leave town, huh?"

"I don't care," the Oogle whimpered.

"You cared enough to follow me, what did you plan to do?"

"I don't know," he cried.

Jobie shook his head, enraged by the Oogle's passive nature. He smacked him upside the head with the brick, sending his perpetrator straight to the ground. Jobie kicked him once in the stomach as he dropped the brick onto his head. He stood alone over two twisted bodies whose blood streamed to the center of the alley.

He nodded. It was in fact time to leave Austin.

SATURDAY, NOVEMBER 7, 1998

Hyde Park
1:27pm

Treva's eyes bulged from the pressure of Vaughn's grip on her neck. His powerful hands clamped her throat viciously, digging deep into the elasticity of her shedding skin. She could feel the darkness penetrating her as she stared into his maniacally twisted eyes. Never before had she seen him so passionate, so alive. Never before had she craved death with such conviction. It was the ultimate sacrifice to her oppressor. Her eyes stared into his, fearless and submissive.

Her larynx felt as if it were collapsing. Her last breath was fading, trapped inside her lungs. The darkness was overwhelming. She looked from side to side, trying to focus on the world that was disappearing in a veil of black fog. She could see the still water in the bathtub behind him. She knew that her dead body would soon be bled into it for his sadistic pleasure. She also knew that her corpse would be tied with bricks and dumped into Town Lake, never to be found.

She hadn't believed him. She didn't think he would actually kill her. Now it was too late.

The day began routinely enough, the clipboard, the notes, the handkerchiefs and the wooden chair...she had watched him turn the porcelain knobs, releasing a steady flow of frosty cold water into the old, deep bathtub. She had noticed there were no syringes anywhere. Her intuition throbbed of danger as he bound her hands for the last time.

She watched him stare at his clipboard, at the disorganized mess of notes on green graph paper. His eyes were glassy, almost rueful. His bearded face was hardened from defeat. She didn't expect him to suddenly tear the notes from the clipboard and discard them into the clear bath water. They floated atop its surface like algae before slowly sinking to the bottom.

He looked down upon Treva, at her rotting flesh. Her skin had tiny rips that ran the length of her body like veins. He had failed. Failed miserably. The serum had taken a life of its own, feeding on the very thing it was designed to save. She would soon be dead, but not soon enough. His failure had eyes, and for as long as she lived, it wasn't merely his secret burden. He shared the cold truth of his declination with his subservient little guinea pig. "You're dying."

"I thought you were going to help me," she sobbed disparagingly. She struggled to free herself. She could feel her skin giving with the tension, tearing like paper. She dissolved her futile efforts immediately. "What are you going to do about this? How can you help me?"

"I can't. I'm simply going to destroy you."

"You already have," she cried.

His empathy singed his stoic mien. He needed her dead, aborted completely from his life. His efforts were a disgrace to his father's name, and it left him emotionally eroded. He couldn't stand to witness his failings. "I will give you the choice of your demise. Consider it merciful. The worst for you is yet to come. I'm offering you a less gruesome death than what lurks in the near future for you. How would you rather die?"

His tart statement was received stolidly, free of panic from its dire implications—she was too dispirited to care anymore. She gave her immediate thoughts: "I want to overdose. Pump me full of dilaudid. I want to die in heaven. Especially since you put me in the hell I'm in. You *owe* it to me."

His compassion quickly crumbled under his steel composure, fueled by the vexing qualities of her insolent personality. "I will drown you, or I will strangle you." He sloshed his hand through the icy bath water. "I want you to die," he confessed with harsh sentiment. "I really do. I want to take your life, I want to finish what I started. I really want that. Quite frankly, I need that."

"You failed, didn't you?" she asked defeatedly. "Your potion poisoned me."

His face tightened with humility and anger. How true her words.

"Cure me," she pleaded. "You will never have to see me again, I'll leave town right now. Right now. I promise."

He sighed. It was beyond his ability and he knew it. He had failed. The realization was catastrophic to the once sturdy foundation of his ego. The fragility of his collapsing spirit was too much for him to bear. "Let's get this over with so I can forget it ever happened." He hovered over her like a vulture, gripping his hands intently. He was ready for the kill.

"That doctor—Doctor Schtepp...this is his fault, isn't it? If I could slaughter that son of a bitch...it's his fault, he did this, didn't he?!"

Richter smiled. He nodded his head, and oh how he wished it were true. "Choose your death."

Tears swelled in her eyes. The ghosts of her past beat her into horrified exhaustion, there was no escape. She was a little girl trapped inside a cage with the cruelest of demons. They violated her body, wearing the guise of her father's face. Her soul was exhausted, she was tired of running. No matter the distance, the brutal nightmares were always waiting to ravage her in sleep. She desperately craved the dilaudid, anything to hush the voices in her head. Her mind was crumbling from the pressure. Her flesh was peeling from her weakened body. Death surrounded her.

"Strangle me," she told him.

Thus was her fate. The darkness consumed her, and the lights faded at the mercy of his hands.

He watched her body fall limp. What clear skin remained on her face had turned a pale shade of blue. He loosened his grip on her neck, watching her body give way to gravity. Lifeless. It appeared that her color was shifting slowly again, returning to pink, but he really couldn't tell—not with the rash that covered her face like a mask of clay. Her lungs appeared to expand slightly, or was it a convulsion deep inside her chest from the organs resisting death?

His posture stiffened. His stomach turned, he felt himself rile from the morbidity of the situation. He couldn't look at her another second. He buttoned his satin emerald shirt to the collar and stepped away from her body. She was like furnishings, no more alive than the chair on which she sat. He walked to the door, grabbing his keys as he left the house to gather his thoughts and to figure out a way to dispose of the body. He walked to his car uneasily. He had done it. He had actually taken her life. Yet he felt nothing. It was a mere fact. He unlocked his car door, letting the thought slip from his mind as he backed the car into the street. A black Plymouth Fury sat by the curb like a topless hearse. Vaughn didn't even notice it, or the raging eyes that peered from within.

6:37pm

Vaughn returned home just as he had left, cold and uninspired. The lingering death was internal.

He threw open the bathroom door where her fleshless body was swathed to the chair. The room was dark, and her figure was little more than a silhouette, but the details were clear enough. There was a foul odor in the air, morbid and grotesque. She seemed to be in an advanced state of decomposition, but with what had happened to her body, he didn't know what to expect. This was death, he concluded, this truly was death. A corpse...there was no rich pool of blood with a warm body, this was death in all its cold grandeur. A stiff, lifeless, rotting corpse.

His heart raced, he felt ill. He stumbled out of the bathroom and to the nearest phone, calling his colleague, the only man he could remotely trust.

"Ronald, I need you!" he exclaimed desperately, breaking the silence of the cold wooden room. "I need to speak with you—now. Please call me immediately. She's dead. Purty's dead. I've killed her... I don't know what to do..."

He collapsed to the bed, slouching nervously. The thought of leaving the room mortified him. He stared forward, almost catatonic. Hours seemed to pass as he sat in cold silence.

The phone rang. He let it ring once, twice...the caller ID showed it to be a cell-phone, but it wasn't Ronald Schtepp's. It was his own. He picked it up without saying a word as he breathed uneasily into the mouthpiece. He could almost feel the tips of bony fingers grazing his spine as the voice of a ghost spoke into his ear: "Surprise...it's me...it's Purty."

He trembled, barely able to hold the phone, shocked and horrified. He visualized her dead body standing in the bathroom, holding his cell phone to her lifeless face. He could see her eyes, glassy and covered with a white film. Practically skinless.

"The doctor is dead—I killed the bastard with your gun, it's at the crime scene."

Disorientation made a swirling mess of his comprehension. He considered all the notes in his laboratory pinning him to a crime he didn't commit. "Who is in the bathroom?" His bark was unnaturally weak. "Who is she?"

Her voice sang out breathy and insipid. "Phaedra."

Flashes of red lights danced down the street to the distant shrill of sirens.

She chuckled innocuously. "I listened to your confession on the doctor's answering machine. You've made this all too easy..."

"Someday..." he snarled. "I will catch and kill you."

"No, you'll never see me again," she corrected him before hanging up.

The flashing lights of police cars surrounded his house. He stood slowly, firmly erect as he gazed across the room to the front window. Several officers apprehensively approached his quiet domain. He stood alone in darkness, watching his life fizzle and sputter before him. The death he had brought on was his own.

This was the finale of his father's legacy.

*   *   *

Jobie stared out at the lonesome highway as the black Fury raced eastward across the Texas border into Louisiana. For all its lofty anticipation, New Orleans was short of a breath away. His hand dangled over the steering wheel as he veered onto the exit ramp into a tiny town named Vinton.

"Where are we going?" Treva wheezed as she scraped her bony fingers along her skeletal cheek. Her speech had worsened. Her bottom lip seemed to be falling from her face.

Jobie pointed straight into the windshield, into the bleak darkness to which they sped. "This way. To get me a rock from Louisiana." He pulled off alongside the ditch some distance off the interstate.

The breeze was algid and moist with the slightest scent of the ocean. Treva inhaled the air deeply in her failing lungs, struggling to accept the death that nipped her heels. She watched Jobie wander into the dark and fumble clumsily, feeling for the perfect stone on the near-frozen earth.

"Jobie," she croaked weakly. "Do you remember when you said that every rock you have reminds you of me?"

His reply was deliberately slow. "Uh-huh." He wandered back to the Fury where he looked down upon her frailty with concern.

"Will you remember this night forever if I ask you to?"

He held out a dark and smooth stone. "You don't even need to ask."

"Jobie...I do know what you've done for me—you once asked if I knew all the things you've done. I do know. I do...I lied to you, though, Jobie. I'm not going to survive this, I'm not going to miraculously heal. I can feel it. My body is dying."

His expression remained fixed like a statue.

"Do you love me?" she exhaled listlessly.

His head slowly lowered, then raised quickly, suddenly. It was more or less a nod.

"Do you?" she repeated, demanding a more absolute response.

"Yeah..."

She smiled peacefully with lips torn like paper. "If I could live my life over again... No one has ever loved me, Jobie, not like you do. Of all the people out there, you chose me. No one has ever done that before." She closed her eyes in serenity while breathing deeply, stumbling into memory. "I loved the sound of rain in the morning while lying in bed. I loved standing in an empty field of snow in the middle of the night—have you ever been in snow?"

He shook his head.

"It's so quiet. You can't imagine. So quiet and peaceful. The snow rolls out like eternity and it collects all sound and light...it glows in the night. It actually glows."

He smiled and listened.

"I loved the smell of chocolate chip cookies when they came out of the oven, and I loved the way my dog looked at me like I was the most amazing creature on the planet. I love the way you look at me, and listen to me. You're the last person I will see in my life, Jobie."

"No," he muttered. "No...you're not dying."

"Silly boy, look at me. I'm falling apart. I once had great skin, and now I don't even have skin! If I was to list my favorite things in life, I'd have to say you were one of them...where were you taking me?"

"We're going to New Orleans. And to the ocean, you're going to sit on the beach with me."

"Oh, I'd love to go..." Her voice sounded ancient and fatigued. "When you go, just know that I'll be there with you. I wouldn't miss it for the world."

"You're not dying, Treva."

"If I ask you to do something for me, would you do it?" she asked.

"Of course."

"The last wish of a dying girl..."

"Don't say that."

"Make love to me, Jobie, please. I've never been loved, I want to know how it feels before I die."

He exhaled deeply and slowly, giving no answer as he clenched his fists in solemn desperation.

"Help me with my pants," she requested.

He knelt beside her, unfastening her loose jeans and pulling them from her body. Her flesh was red and glossy like meat in a butcher's window. She reached up to his face and pulled him down upon her by his ears. He fell on top of her slippery body and nuzzled his face into her slick-textured neck. He closed his eyes and imagined her riding on the freight train that carried them through the desert to Texas. He could see the sun burning over her shoulder like a fiery plum, blending purely with her once beautiful hair. She pulled his kilt up to his waist as he squeezed his eyes tightly together. She spread her legs and he slipped inside her easily, gracefully as if they were an old feeble couple. He could feel the resistance of her flesh, shredding and tearing and unifying. He held her tightly, holding her gently as she breathed heavily into his ear, "Kill me." She grabbed his hips to keep him from stopping. "This is how I want to die, with you inside me. Please, I'll be dead soon...I'll die miserable and alone, but to die like this—do you understand? What better way to go?"

"I can't kill you."

"If you love me—if you *truly* love me, you will kill me."

He hesitated, feeling the cold clamoring of his senses.

"You won't be alone," she assured him with stunted breath. "I'll never leave you. We'll live forever. We were meant to." She looked into his eyes, bleeding the peace into him. "It'd be the best gift you could give me. I'm not afraid, I'm ready to go. I do want to go...I'm tired, Jobie. I'm so tired. Help me. Please."

"I'm not ready for you to go."

"I'm dying, I have no choice. It'd be a mercy killing, it'd be out of love." She reached into the pocket of her pants that lie at her side on the floorboard. She pulled out the blade and placed it in his hands. He clutched it in the faint light, staring at its smooth metal surface. "Cum inside me," she beckoned. "Then kill me."

He pushed his cock deep inside her, thrusting quickly with vigor as his heart froze in his chest. The loneliness overwhelmed him, it broke reality to the present in a screeching halt that burned his ears. He could feel his heart beating furiously in his chest as he savored their final togetherness. It was better than any moment in his life, the beginning and the end. The best and worst wrapped in one single stroke of the brush.

His body quaked violently as he exploded inside her like a fountain. He raised his hands to his head as he gripped the knife firmly in his gaunt hands. He visualized the sun and the desert and the train...and the knife collapsed through her chest, into her heart. The blood spilled onto the floorboard as she gasped desperately, "Don't forget me." He could taste the blood on her lips, he could feel the convulsing muscles quake inside her vagina as she fell slowly to silence, succumbing to death.

He sat at her side for hours, talking to her body and crying, sharing his life until the sun lit the sky like cold grape juice. As he drove his love to New Orleans, his body felt like glass—fragile and transparent. Her head rested on his lap peacefully as he imagined her spirit following high overhead in the stars, watching him, protecting him. He would never be alone again.

Also available from Layman Books by Charles Romalotti...

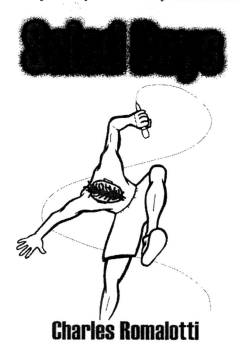

Charles Romalotti

Salad Days keeps your heart pumping high-octane gasoline and your emotions running high. Romalotti's debut novel is quite an accomplishment...a great book.
- Maximum RockNRoll

A fast-paced, engrossing, and thoroughly enjoyable read.
- Ramsey Kanaan, President of AK Press distribution

One of the finest books I've ever read.
- punkrockreviews.com

I cannot explain how much I thoroughly enjoyed this book. No kidding, this is *good* reading.
- Boots fanzine

Charles Romalotti's debut novel is an excellent first stab at punk authorship.
- Willamette Week (Portland, Oregon)

Salad Days...how things were when it all really mattered.
- LA Weekly

Charles Romalotti is the author of *Salad Days*. His
second novel, *Rash* is currently in the process of
being developed into a motion picture by an
independent American filmmaker. Romalotti lives
in Austin, Texas and is currently working on two
novels—*Talon* and *The Stickler*. *Talon*, which is
the sequel to *Rash*, is due out late 2002.